The entertainment field has been no stranger to Paul Stanton over the years; having worked in both theatre and television. He has written numerous plays, novels and children's books, before finally dedicating himself to what he considers to be his magnum opus: *A Festive Juxtaposition.* After much input it is a work Paul is finally happy with (having rewritten it a total of fifteen times) and regards it as a 'little Christmas ditty' that hopefully people will like and warm to.

I would like to dedicate this book to my loving wife, Julie, who has endured and loved me for many years, and also my friend, Johanna, for her continual willingness to read my efforts and to give me much needed feedback. And of course, Peter, my lifelong friend and staunch ally in the continual fight against literary incompetence.

Paul R Stanton

A Festive Juxtaposition

Austin Macauley Publishers™

LONDON • CAMBRIDGE • NEW YORK • SHARJAH

A CIP catalogue record for this title is available from the British Library.

ISBN 9781398494244 (Paperback)
ISBN 9781398494251 (ePub e-book)

www.austinmacauley.com

First Published 2022
Austin Macauley Publishers Ltd®
1 Canada Square
Canary Wharf
London
E14 5AA

I would like to take this opportunity to thank Austin Macauley Publishers for giving me the chance of allowing the general public to view my work. My heartfelt thanks.

Table of Content

Chapter One: The First of the Dispossessed Nigel   11

Chapter Two: The Second of the Dispossessed
Old Meg   26

Chapter Three: The Third of the Dispossessed
The Professor   38

Chapter Four: The Fourth, Fifth and Sixth of the
Dispossessed Ed, Barry and Razors   50

Chapter Five: The Seventh of the Dispossessed May   65

Chapter Six: The Eighth, Ninth and Tenth of the
Dispossessed Laz, Dominic and Lucy   79

Chapter Seven: The Eleventh of the
Dispossessed Miriam   90

Chapter Eight: The Twelfth of the Dispossessed
Michael Asquith   99

Chapter Nine: The Thirteenth of the Dispossessed
Rev. Adrian Noble   111

Chapter Ten: A Brief Aside   122

Chapter Eleven: The Last of the Dispossessed Peggy   139

Chapter Twelve: The Final Farewell   160

Chapter Thirteen: And What Happened After   163

Chapter One
The First of the
Dispossessed Nigel

It was on Christmas Eve at precisely 6.27 pm Greenwich
Mean Time that the Devil suddenly appeared at Charing Cross
Station. His mode of transport in order to arrive there hadn't
been by the established method of travel, that being by either
train, taxi or foot, no nothing so mundane. He had merely
materialised out of thin air, as he was wont to do on occasions
such as this. One minute there was empty space and the next
minute there was the Devil. Of course, he didn't look anything
like you might imagine the Devil to look: and what I mean by
this was that there was no pitch-fork, no horns, no cloven
hoofs, no sulphurous miasma to give any clear indication as
just to who he might be. If anything, he looked pretty
ordinary, mundane and most commonplace and fitted into his
surroundings quite nicely.

He stood tall and lean and was immaculately turned out, standing well over six feet in his highly polished patent black leather shoes. He always took great pride in his appearance.

His chiselled aquiline features looked as though they had been carved from granite, which gave him an intensely piercing look. He sported a short, black, well-groomed goatee beard, giving the starkest impression of what you might assume the devil would look like if he had taken the trouble to assume human form and you had inadvertently bumped into him by chance in the street one day. And of course in that assumption, you would have been perfectly correct.

The weather was unseasonably cold for the time of year, and it had been snowing heavily for the best part of the afternoon, causing feathery white drifts to amass in large white swathes amongst the many doorways and ingresses of the old city. Stepping out from the confines of the station concourse, the Devil stopped briefly for a moment and gazed upwards into the night sky, breathing in the crisp night air in an overly emphatic capacious intake of oxygen. His over emphasised exhalation immediately turned into a swathe of evanescent vapour, disappearing into the surrounding night almost before it was exhaled. He looked about him and smiled a broad, knowing smile; it was a smile that hid many undisclosed thoughts and intentions, a smile that spoke of one who is party to every last secret – no matter how well hidden. It was a good moment for him. He felt that he was coming home again. In truth, he felt thoroughly alive.

Looking up, his attention was taken in by the Amba Hotel. It never ceased to amaze him just how ignorant the majority of Londoners were of this magnificent edifice. In fact, it was true to say that the greater proportion of those who used

Charing Cross station on a daily basis gave it little or no thought at all, preferring to believe that it was simply an integral part of the station itself. It was in fact quite a wonderful hotel, albeit a little faded now, having been opened just a month after Abraham Lincoln had been assassinated. It had survived the blitz during the second world war, which much of the old city had not – and of course not forgetting the much greater competition for trade in later years. Still, it stood as a continuing stalwart against the continuing transformation of the old metropolis, remaining a continuing bastion against the seething metamorphosis brought on by the very nature of time itself and he loved it.

The gentle snowflakes flurried, eddied and whirled, dancing in their oddly curious coruscation, before finally descending to earth where their individuality was lost amongst their earlier brethren.

It had to be said, of all the times of the year, Christmas time had always been his personal favourite. There was something intrinsically right about it all he thought – the lights, the tinsel, the smells, the decorations, the general bonhomie, the warm glow and the universal good humour that was to be discovered in virtually all walks of life at this time. There was, he thought, nothing quite like it. He was, by choice, a bon vivant and Christmas time fitted his tastes all too perfectly. A moment's reflection made him realise that the last time it had snowed in the city like this was Christmas Eve 2010. There had been work aplenty to do that night and tonight he knew was to be no exception.

With that in mind, he turned up the collar on his astrakhan coat, clapped his gloved hands together with a purpose and stepped forth into the glowing and pulsating night. Naturally, he was immured to the cold. That went without saying and was to be expected; he was the Devil after all. This was his realm and he could do with it whatever he liked. And it had to be said he generally did just that. He strode forward with clear intent. He was a man on a mission. Though it would have been more exact to have said 'he was the Devil on a mission'. The cold rime crunched loudly beneath his size ten shoes. *A fitting sound,* he thought. There was nothing quite like the sound of freshly driven snow being crunched underfoot. It always gave off such a myriad of different thoughts, hopes and expectations. And they were all associated with this time of year. It was a magical time.

He once again took a deep lungful of the cold night air and then set off on his quest. Leaving the hotel forecourt, he immediately bore right and turned into Villiers Street, stopping but for a moment to gaze at the multitude of Christmas lights that were displayed all along The Strand, sparkling as they were like a million iridescent, multi-facetted highly polished gems. "Wonderful," he remarked to himself, "truly wonderful," before continuing on his way. As he peered along the street, his eye was surprisingly drawn to the sight of himself standing just across the other side of the street. This was something he hadn't expected at all and the image of himself standing there staring back at him momentarily threw him off-guard. What was going on? His alter-ego gave a cursory nod as if to say 'no fuss', to which the Devil gave the same in reply. Then they both moved on without a word. Whatever it was, he would undoubtedly find out soon enough, right now there were other matters more pressing to which he had to attend to.

Within a few strides, he had encountered the first of his many quarries that night (and there were to be many). Shivering within the confines of a shop doorway, there resided an unkempt man of early years. He was surrounded by all manner of things: bags, clothes, flattened bits of cardboard, pieces of cloth and a sleeping bag – anything that might provide some minor comfort against the awful chill of the night air. And it was chill indeed – cold enough to freeze you through to the very marrow of your bones. The temperature had dropped like a stone to well below freezing on this rather special night of the year, so the young man's attempts at this particular undertaking had been unfortunately mostly in vain. He sat shivering in a most pathetic way, reflecting miserably upon his lot in life and cursing everyone and everything for it.

Now, as a brief, but important aside: Villiers Street runs adjacent to Charing Cross station, which in turn runs all the way down to Embankment Station. And beyond this lies the River Thames. Throughout the year, the street attracts many homeless people of all ages, mainly due to its being off the main thoroughfare. It seemingly provides the odd secluded niche here and there, where the dispossessed can usually find a place to rest up and more often than not spend the night. Most of the shops that run along its length were closed up for the holiday, their tradesfolk now all set about doing different Christmassy pursuits. Apart from a solitary pub and a couple of fast food outlets, there was little or no activity at all, save for the occasional couple or the odd individual that used the street as a cut-through, or those who had imbibed a little too much festive libation and were trying to find their way home again.

But we digress. This story is about the Devil and his particular pursuits and purposes upon this most holiest of nights. Treading with measured strides, he silently approached the young man, the same young man whom fate had seemed to have so sorely neglected. The same young man who now sat freezing in a shop doorway. His grin did not diminish for an instant. There it sat etched upon his face in total splendour, as if cocking-a-snook at the cold and impoverishment all in one go.

"Good evening," he offered in his semi-stentorian voice, (choosing to limit himself a tad as a mark of respect for the time of year).

The poor unfortunate raised his head but briefly against the billowing snow, his teeth remorselessly beating a tattoo against the frozen marrow in his bones and stammered in an ill-mannered tone.

"W-What do you want?"

"A brief chat, Nigel, a brief chat, nothing more," replied the Devil cordially and promptly took a small three-legged stool from seemingly out of thin air and sat down upon it before the homeless individual.

The young man gazed at his new companion dubiously, not knowing quite to make of him.

"H-How do you know my name?" he asked, and a look of sudden dread passed across his features.

Unabashed and choosing to continue with his disarming smile, the Devil replied, "Oh, I know everything about you, Nigel. Absolutely everything that is worth knowing. But before we proceed, how about we warm you up a trifle? It's terribly cold at the moment, don't you know? Here, take this. I think you will like it. It's a rather special weave. Specially woven to retain the heat, or so they tell me. Not that I'd know. A terrific boon against this kind of weather mind." And so saying, he produced a large blanket from behind his back and handed it across to the poor young man. Nigel took it gladly, not giving a hoot as to its origin and quickly wrapped it about his person; straight away feeling all the better for it.

"How's that? Better, I bet?" asked the Devil, still sporting a beatific smile.

Nigel nodded thankfully, warming to his new companion.

"Yeah, that's great. Thanks. Much better. Appreciate it. Can I keep it?"

This time, it was the Devil's turn to nod.

"Naturally, you can keep it, my boy. It goes without saying, don't you know? A gift at Christmas should be both useful and given with charitable intentions and with no thought of gain, isn't that right? It's what Christmas is all about. You may keep it for as long as you may require it and even longer should the need arise. It is yours."

"Huh, then I'll be having it for a long time then," grunted Nigel despondently.

"We shall see about that my friend, we shall most definitely see about that," replied the Devil, all the while retaining his merry mien to the last. "It's Christmas, Nigel, and miracles often happen at this time of year, or so they say. And THEY are rarely wrong in my experience. And I've certainly heard of the odd miracle myself here and there. Why it's a time when miracles happen, my friend."

"Huh. Miracles aren't for the likes of me. They are for others," responded Nigel sullenly. "I'm cursed."

This news made the Devil shake his head in bold and obvious disagreement.

"Ah, Nigel, Nigel. Be of good cheer and have a little faith, my boy. Why, this is the season of optimism and goodwill to all men. You'll find that just a smidgeon of faith can very often move mountains."

Nigel did not look convinced by the remark and averted his gaze, believing that his companion was very wrong about that. Feeling that the moment required him to say something, he asked, "You haven't told me how you know my name. Are you a social worker or something? If you are, then it's a bit late in the day. Christmas Eve and all, I mean."

The Devil nodded once again.

"A social worker of sorts. Yes, I suppose I could be called that. We work all year round, Christmas Eve being no exception to that." Then taking a ream of papers from inside his coat pocket he opened them out and began to read from them with a practised and professional manner. "Nigel Boscombe, born 17 April 1997, Bradley. Lived with parents until the age of eighteen. Troubled schooling. Constantly getting into bother. Oh dear oh dear. Left school at sixteen. Failed to keep down a job for more than a few months. Diagnosed with *Apathetic Indolence* in May 2010. Offered counselling and treatment. Local GP arranged an appointment for you – which apparently you duly chose not to turn up for. Finally, after a long running set of altercations between yourself, your sister and parents you were asked to leave. You have been homeless ever since. My oh my. It doesn't make for good reading, does it?"

For a brief moment, Nigel mulled things over before finally responding.

"I wasn't to blame for any of that," he said bitterly. "It wasn't my fault. None of it was. It was all their doing!" The response seemed to emanate from the depths of his soul. The Devil listened and then nodded.

"No, in my experience, those who are culpable rarely are to blame," he replied. "Ironic though, isn't it? I mean, if only you had seen fit to bend a little all those years ago and possibly observe the other side of the coin once in a while, then you wouldn't be here at this particular juncture in time would you, I mean sitting in the freezing cold and the snow talking to me now. Incidentally, lest I forget, I have a thermos of hot soup here for you. It should go part-ways to warming you up a little. Here."

From inside his coat, the Devil conjured up a thermos and handed it to Nigel.

"Oh… Thanks."

The Devil smiled once more.

"A trifle, Nigel, a mere bagatelle I can assure you. A little act of kindness is all it takes to make the world seem a rosier place, if only for a short time. You will find that that particular thermos has some unusual properties. It holds quite a lot in fact. You may find that you cannot finish it all in one sitting, or even two for that matter."

Nigel removed the lid and poured himself a hefty measure of the steaming liquid. It smelt like heaven to him. As he began to sip on it gently, he felt its revitalising properties begin to flow through his body. He felt warmed by it, cheered and was beginning to feel his extremities once again. While he drank silently, the Devil looked skywards, once again appreciating the ever-falling snow.

"It's beautiful, isn't it?" he said, more rhetorically than anything else.

Nigel sipped his hot soup, not even bothering to look up. It wasn't something he found beautiful at all. He found it utterly horrendous, and he hated it.

"It's not so beautiful if you're homeless," he grumbled. "It's hellish."

The Devil looked on and gave a wicked grin.

"Hellish, Nigel? Hellish, did you say? My my, you couldn't be more wrong – and believe me I'm talking from personal experience here. There's nothing hellish about this at all, and you take my word for it."

The Devil's remark was totally lost on the young man, who continued to drink his soup miserably. At last, he spoke, "If you've come to try and persuade me to enter a shelter or something, then you're wasting your time. I won't go, I won't. They're worse than sleeping out here. And believe me that's saying something. The last time I was in one of those places, I had what few belongings I possessed stolen – and that included my shoes! And someone threatened me with a knife. No thank you, you can keep shelters. I'll stay here."

The Devil appeared altogether horrified at the suggestion.

"Shelter? Oh heaven forbid!" he agreed. "A shelter! Dreadful places. Awful! I am totally with you there all the way, my boy. They should all be closed down in my opinion. I personally wouldn't be seen dead in one, and that's saying something. And neither should you in my opinion. No, very wise. Prudence tells you to remain out here in the elements and the sub-zero temperatures, where you will probably die from hypothermia. It's no bad thing to want to die for your principles. It's to be admired in fact. Truly admired. The graveyards are overflowing with people who have done just that. No, I go along with you wholeheartedly, Nigel. To hell with them all I say! Saying that, of course, there's also a lot to be said for remaining alive and rectifying your past mistakes. Good karma and what not."

Between mouthfuls of the soup, Nigel considered his odd benefactor, not knowing what to make of him in the slightest. Then, having given the matter a great deal of thought, replied.

"My only mistake was not leaving home earlier than I did. They deserve everything they get. I have no remorse about what I did."

The Devil took on board the young man's comments.

"You know, Nigel, Marcus Aurelius once remarked 'The greatest revenge is not to be likened unto them'. And oh was he so right about that. He was a very clever man you know."

"Was he? Well, I've never heard of him," replied Nigel. "And I don't know what that means anyway."

"No, and why should you my young friend? Why should you? Your family – I bet they didn't understand you – did they?"

"Too damn right they didn't! Not one of them. It didn't matter what went wrong, you could guarantee I would always end up getting the blame for it. I got fed up with the whole thing."

"Ah, you may take my word for that, Nigel, when I say I completely understand where you are coming from. There's no one walking the earth at present that is more castigated and misunderstood than I am, believe you me. No, I think perhaps you're far better off without them."

Nigel nodded in total agreement.

"I've been much happier since I left."

The Devil perused the young man at length with an altogether quizzical look and then made great show of doing the same to his surroundings.

"Yes, I have to say I can see the appeal of rotting slowly away in a shop doorway. No friends, no money, no hope, no future. The only thing to comfort you in your lonely days being your misplaced loathing of those who have tolerated your abuse and exploitation for years. It veritably makes it all pale into insignificance in comparison – don't you think? Are you aware that the celebrated Dr Johnson once said '*When a man is tired of London then he is tired of life?*' Of course he wasn't quite in the same predicament that you currently find yourself in now, but there's a useful moral to the story if you look for it."

Nigel began to fidget uncomfortably, feeling the Devil's words were a little too close to the truth for his liking, and despite the blanket and the soup, he wished he would go away.

"What is your point?" he asked finally, sounding a little more irritable than he would have liked considering the kindness he had been shown.

The Devil's response was immediate, aggressive and altogether brutal. His demeanour and appearance instantly changed, his eyes began to smoulder and glow with a near hellish infernal radiance. His form seemed to take on an almost gargantuan bearing as the general festive background melody faded inextricably away. A faint wisp of sulphur blew up, but was then lost almost as quickly amongst the ever-falling snow.

"It's very simple, Nigel," he began. ***"Your present situation has been brought about by none other than yourself! You spend your time constantly sitting in a*** *pathetic morbid stupor, drowning in a quagmire of self-inflicted self-pity; constantly looking outwards for people to blame for your earthly plight; family, friends, people in the street and society in general. It's forever someone else's fault and never yours! Open your eyes my rend ad see what is staring you in the face – open your eyes before it is too late! The truth can set you FREE."*

For a moment, a petrified Nigel did not respond to the Devil's accusations and all too accurate implications. He looked on in an admixture of speechless awe and terror, not daring to speak, not able to speak. Then, just as quickly as it had come, the Devil's manner and appearance returned to what it had been previously, leaving a smiling benign character in its stead.

"It's t…too late for me now," Nigel eventually blurted out in his own defence. "There's nowhere for me to go! Nowhere! There's never anywhere for people like me to go. We have no hope."

The Devil's smile seemed to grow ever wider and he began to roar with laughter, a laughter that was unmistakable in its honesty and good humour.

"Nonsense, my boy! Utter hogwash! There is always hope, even when all hope appears to have gone. And as for having nowhere to go, why I don't think I have ever heard such a greater misnomer – why, Nigel you can go home! Home and everything that it stands for and that it represents!"

It was now Nigel's turn to laugh heartily, but this was not born out of happiness or joy, but more an embittered, cynical laugh that seemed to echo from the very depths of his wretched soul.

"I have no home – not unless you can call this home." He gestured to the small pile of things that surrounded him. "This is now all I have. Things don't ever change for the likes of me. They never have and they never will. This is my whole life now."

"Twaddle, claptrap, complete and utter baloney!" roared the Devil. "Why, I was only speaking with your parents this very morning – and I repeat – this very morning! And they can't wait for your return. Beside themselves, they were with both worry and joy in the knowledge that you would be coming home once again."

Nigel, now completely mystified, looked on in utter bewilderment and perplexity.

"What do you mean? You can't have spoken with my parents," he said. "That's just not possible."

"Not possible? Why, anything is possible. And I think you will find that I can do a lot more than that," rejoined the Devil. "A whole lot more in fact. See here."

And so saying he placed his hand within the confines of his coat and pulled out an envelope, which he handed to Nigel with a flourish.

"In there, you will find a train ticket to Bradley, along with some money to get you back on your feet. Your train leaves in precisely nine minutes. I heartily suggest that you make sure you are on it. Your parents will be waiting for you at the other end."

What was this? Surely this couldn't be happening? A numbness crept over the young man, his senses failing to take on board precisely what had just taken place.

"What? What do you mean? My family? But how?" he uttered incredulously.

The Devil merely nodded.

"Yes, your family. They are waiting for you at the other end. As we speak in fact. Well, go on Nigel – Hop to it! Time waits for no man!"

"But—" began Nigel, only to be stopped in his tracks by the Devil's finger, which he now held aloft in a commanding and authoritative manor that brooked no question at all.

"Go now, or there will be Hell to pay!" he said. "Trust me. If you don't go now, you will miss that train!"

Without another word, Nigel collected together what he could of his few belongings and began to move hurriedly towards the station. Then stopping briefly, he turned and called back.

"Who are you?"

The Devil mused for a second, smiled and then bowed low.

"Appellations I have many, Nigel. However, you may call me Nick," he said.

Nigel ran off, waving and dropping items as he went.

"Thank you, Nick," he yelled back, before disappearing into Charing Cross Station.

The Devil stood watching the young man go, pleased with his initial efforts. A good start he thought. Yes, a very good start to his night's work, but there was still plenty to do.

"When you are in Hell, only the Devil can point the way out," he intoned quietly, before turning and making his way down Villiers Street.

Chapter Two
The Second of the
Dispossessed Old Meg

In the distance, a random church clock could be heard chiming the hour. Its measured, unhurried peals slowly and irrevocably faded into the chilly ether. There could also be heard the bright heartening sound of Christmas Carols that floated merrily on the wind. Pausing for a brief second, in order to take in the joyful sounds, the Devil listened intently, tapping his foot lightly in time with their lively rhythm. The echoing cadence slowly died away, leaving once again the general Christmas hubbub caused by those out to make the most of the time of year.

"If I say it a thousand times," muttered the Devil to himself good humouredly, "I'll never tire of the sound. It's wonderful, simply wonderful."

His blissful reverie was unfortunately broken by the sound of two young men. They were both dressed in Santa suits and had just that very moment issued forth from a bar across the way. It was obvious that they were quite intoxicated. Spotting the Devil, they both stopped and began to regale him, both with obscenities and Christmas greetings simultaneously.

"Hoy lofty!" the one shouted loudly. "I said Merry Christmas! You mutton-jeff or something? Eh? I said are you listening to me! Where's your Christmas spirit? Hoy! You!"

The Devil stopped and stared across the street at the two young men, his eyes narrowing almost imperceptibly, but narrow they did.

"Be watchful. The ice is particularly precarious underfoot on that stretch of pavement," he called brightly in response. "I suggest you be careful how you walk. Oh, and a very Merry Christmas to you both." And saying that, he moved on without giving them a second thought. The two drunken individuals took no more notice of him, being already tired of their own particular humour, and did the same. Or at least that was their intention. Having taken a single step in the direction in which they were heading, they both slipped heavily upon the frozen ground (as predicted). Their ensuing screams filled the air; the first complaining loudly of having broken his wrist, whilst the other held his bleeding head, having cracked it with some force on the side of a concrete step he had collided with as he had fallen.

"Will people never learn?" the Devil could be heard muttering wilfully to himself as he strode ever onwards.

In next to no time, he encountered an underpass on his right; this was Hungerford Lane and it ran from Villiers Street and in to Craven Street beyond. This was the very place where a very young Charles Dickens had spent much of his formative years filling tins with boot polish in order to make a few shillings for his family. His father, having been consigned to the Marshelsea Prison for debts owed, was unable to provide the necessary wherewithal and the onus had been left to a very young Charles. Like many brave stoics, he had weathered the storm and finally made good. And, as they say, the rest had become history. My, how things had changed thought the Devil.

Despite there being various lights left on by the shopkeepers, the lighting was still rather gloomy and dismal, with much of Hungerford Lane, due to the lateness of the hour, being in deep shadow. The Devil didn't care a jot for that. He knew precisely where he was heading and duly pressed on. After travelling no more than fifty yards at the most, a female voice rang out in a shrilly tone.

"Why speak of the devil!" it called. "I know you! I do! I say, I know you!"

The Devil stopped and focused his attention in the direction from where the voice had originated. It came from what at first appeared to be nothing more than a large pile of assorted rags and other pieces of odd detritus; it was placed all in what resembled a semi-organised heap, which lay to the side of a baker's shop. Sitting in the middle of all this assortment was an elderly woman. She was clad in two over-coats, a woolly hat, thick gloves and a scarf that was wrapped circuitously about her neck. Her appearance gave the semblance of a large puffed-up bird that was firmly ensconced upon its nest.

She pointed a finger towards the Devil and then repeated loudly.

"Yes, I know you all right. I've seen you before I have!"

"Hello, Meg," said the Devil with a smile. "You old curmudgeon. Long time no see."

"Well, I never. I say, well I never. It's been too long. Far too long," replied the elderly woman. "Where have you been all this time? It must be, ooh let me think, years now, it must be, yes years. I can't even remember how long it has been."

Producing the small three-legged stool that he had used earlier, when chatting to Nigel, the Devil placed it before Meg and sat down upon it.

"Indeed it is, Meg, indeed it is. It certainly has been years. I don't get back here as often as I'd like to. I have so much to do. My work keeps me rather occupied. I must say though that you are looking well on its mind, despite the passing of the years. Not a day older I do believe. And if I was honest, I would say that I'm very surprised you remember me at all, very surprised indeed."

Meg chuckled. It was a hearty chuckle that despite her situation spoke of merriment and a good spirit.

"Course I remember you. You was kind to old Meg, though I was a fair bit younger then. I remember things like that. Not too many folks nowadays show you any kindness, not when you're on the streets that is. They just don't care, you see? Too much to think about in this modern world, what with all these new gadgets and finga-mathings they've got. Too much to do. Human nature, that's what it is. They don't usually give you the time of day. But you was different to the rest of 'em. You was different to old Meg. Yes, I remember that very well. Stuck in my head it did. You showed Meg kindness – and if I remember rightly, you brought me a little gift too. Most unexpected it was. Much appreciated though. Mind, it was a long time ago. You've probably forgotten all about that now."

Meg said this in a rather coy way and smiled expectantly as she said it, her face turned just enough to one side to give the impression of being both hopeful and mischievous. The Devil laughed uproariously. A laugh that spoke of nothing less than unmistakable joviality and merriment and one that fitted perfectly well with the season. It was an altogether glorious laugh.

"You incorrigible old rogue!" he roared. And then from inside his coat he removed a bottle. "A trifle remiss of me, Meg. I'm forgetting my manners. This is the time of year when it is expected to come laden with offerings, so I must assume that you mean this."

Meg's wrinkled face beamed and lit up, as would a child's on Christmas morning, as she took the bottle and perused it lovingly.

"Oooh, look at that. Best gin," she cooed, caressing the bottle affectionately. "My favourite tipple – merely to keep the cold out! You're an angel, that's what you are, you're a bleedin' angel."

The Devil raised an eyebrow at the inference and smiled thoughtfully.

"Yes, I was once – a long time ago," he casually replied. "A lot of water has passed beneath the bridge since then. Too much in fact. But, as they say, it never pays to complain of one's lot in life. It's better to simply get on and grin and bear it. And we all have our part to play in the scheme of things, don't we? Here, let me do that."

Seeing that Meg was having trouble removing the top to the gin bottle, he took it from her and quickly performed the deed.

"There. Now I do believe I have a couple of small glasses on my person somewhere. Just give me a moment to locate them."

With a sweep of his hand, two small beakers materialised from out of nowhere. Filling both to the brim, he handed one to Meg, who proceeded to take a large sip of the wondrous nectar.

"Oooh, that's a drop of the good stuff," she announced. "Goes straight to the spot. Doesn't burn as it goes down, not like some of the cheaper muck you can get. Lovely and smooth it is."

The Devil muttered that for the price they charged for it was hardly surprising. Not that it had cost him a penny. Then, nothing ever did.

"A toast," he declared, raising his tumbler. "To Meg. May she continue to live a long and prosperous existence and be forever in the thrall of the fortunes of fate."

They clinked their tumblers and wished one another a very happy Christmas.

"So," asked the Devil when they had done. "What have you been up to since I saw you last? There must be lots to tell me. I expect you to fill me in as they say with all the gory details."

Meg thought for a moment, wrinkling up her brow as she did so.

"Oh, this and that," she offered after a moment. "Used to be based around St Martins for years. People knew me there you see. Always had me regulars. They'd help me when they could. But the council's cracked down since then; cracked down a bit on people dossing around there. You get moved on a lot, if you gets my meanin'. But I've got no complaints, not since I found this place. Here – put your hand down here. Go on, just here." She indicated a large metal grill upon which she was sitting. The Devil removed his glove and did so. A warmup-draft met his fingers.

"Very nice, Meg. It reminds me a bit of home to be honest." He noted.

"Yes, all mod cons here and no mistake. This place is a very select cake shop durin' the day. Makes all their own stuff I believe. Mind you, nice prices too. I certainly couldn't afford 'em. Dirty big ovens they've got. Gives off heat for hours after they've all gone home. I found this place quite by accident a few months ago. Of course, it wasn't so cold then. But I remembered it; so when it dropped a bit I was here like a shot. Wouldn't move now. Not for anything. I couldn't move. It's bleedin' cold out there Freeze to death I would in next to no time."

The Devil assured her that while he drew breath her place here was forever safe. Meg grinned and continued, "I'm not as strong as I was. I find it difficult to get about you see. And I've got no family left now. They've all gone. Every one of 'em. Either died or moved away. And those still livin' don't get in touch anymore. They looks down their noses at me. Of course, when my Albert passed away things took a turn for the worst. Found it hard I did, and the Council didn't help. Useless bleedin' lot. Didn't give me a penny, despite me havin' worked all me life. Not a bean. Made me homeless they did. I had nowhere to go. Had to go and live on the streets…I didn't want to. I had no choice…"

Meg lapsed into a solemn brooding silence. Taking her hand gently, the Devil began to talk of more positive things.

"We must try and be a little more optimistic Meg. Life often appears as though there is no hope left and that things are closing in from all sides – but the tide will always inevitably turn for the good. You may trust me on this."

Shaking her head, Meg let out a long sigh.

"Good fortune is never for the likes of us on the streets," she said bitterly echoing Nigel's words. "Those with the money hangs onto it. Always have. Can't blame 'em mind. I'd do the same. But I do know is they don't give it to us. They're the ones with all the luck. They say the Devil looks after his own, and no mistake. That's what they say. And it's bleedin' true. Old Nick does an all, God bless him!"

"Not always, Meg, not always," replied the Devil. "And, it has to be said, to give the Devil his due, he has to contend with more things than you can even begin to imagine. But let us not become morose – it's Christmas Eve and things of a miraculous nature can often happen at this time of year. I often impart this bit of wisdom to people I meet, but they rarely take heed of it."

His optimism made her laugh.

"I can't see me-self being invited to stay at the Savoy by some posh nob, Christmas Eve or not, can you? And I don't see anyone providing me with a full Christmas dinner tomorrow neither. What I've got is some sausage rolls I bought earlier – and they're gone passed their sell by date. Bit stale and a bit dry, but they'll just have to do. It's too cold to move far away from here. I'll make do with what I has. I'm not complainin', don't get me wrong. There's a lot out there a lot worse off than me. Poor sods."

"What if I told you I could provide you with some shelter over the Christmas period, Meg?" he offered. "It would be warm and secure and there would even be a Christmas dinner thrown in? How does that sound?"

The proposal seemed to throw Meg somewhat. She thought about it at length.

"Well, I dunno. How could you do that? And anyway, even if you could I'd lose my spot here if I left it. I wouldn't want that. Nothing to come back to you see. I'd be worse off."

The Devil shook his head.

"'Ah, we are our very own devils; we drive ourselves out of our own Eden'," he quoted.

Meg looked at him quizzically. "Eh?" she asked, not understanding so much as a word of what he was talking about.

"Goethe," he replied. "Not that it has any great significance. Don't mind me, Meg. You may rest assured that should you take me up on my offer, I give you my solemn word that no one will take your place here. It will remain safe and sound awaiting your return. I promise."

Meg eyed him a mite suspiciously.

"Go on then, swear now. Likes you mean it," she said.

The Devil rose, spread his arms wide and bowed graciously.

"May I extol the truth till the day I die, and be forever damned in hell If I tell a lie!" he replied.

The offer was tempting, there was little doubt about that. Meg deliberated for some moments. Warmth, food, company – and she wouldn't lose out here if she accepted. What was the catch? There was always a catch. You never got anything for nothing in this world. If nothing else, she had learnt that from painful experience.

"Where is this place anyway?" she wanted to know, as she was still not totally convinced.

"Not far," he said. "A stone's throw at most. Trust me, Meg."

Placing a finger against her bottom lip thoughtfully, she asked him, "Could I have another drop of that gin, just to think it over like? Gin always helps me to think, I finds."

The Devil took up the bottle, swiftly poured another two glasses of mother's ruin and handed one to Meg. She drank it down in one and then after a moment said, "But how would I get there? I mean I can't walk far these days, me legs won't let me – and it's treacherous on that ice. I'd break me bleedin' neck tryin'."

Retaking his seat, the Devil patted her knee and smiled sympathetically.

"Just say the word, Meg and your taxi awaits." Turning, he gestured towards a large black vehicle parked further up the street. "I will ensure that you are taken there safely, with all your belongings, and when you chose to return, I will also make certain that you are brought here to this very same spot. I can't say more. Is that a bargain?"

Meg looked puzzled and not to say a little unsure. Though she did appear to be warming to the idea.

"Why would you do all this for me? It don't make no sense. I ain't nobody. I ain't never bin nobody. I'm nothin."

"Each and every one of us is somebody, Meg. Some people just don't get the breaks. And anyway, it's very good Karma. Cast your bread upon the waters and all that. Well, what do you say? I can have my man here collect and drive you to your destination in less than fifteen minutes. You'd be warm, secure and in very good company."

Tempting as it all seemed Meg still wasn't completely convinced by the offer. No one ever gave her anything and she was only too aware that you never got anything for nothing in this world.

"Is it safe?" she wanted to know. "I mean, would I be in safe hands there?"

"As safe as a proverbial house, my dear. Take my word for it, there's no place safer in the whole of London."

"And what would I be travelling to? I ain't going to no hostel! I'd sooner die than go there. Worst places going they are."

"Yes, so people keep telling me," agreed the Devil. "But your fears are unfounded, never fear. This is a small hotel of my own procurement, furnished to my own tastes. You would have your own room with everything you need."

The old woman shook her head.

"I don't have a lot of money. I mean I couldn't pay much. Got a bit put by, but it isn't much."

The Devil rose from the stool, knowing his work there was very soon coming to an end. Raising a hand towards the darkened vehicle at the end of the street, he smiled benignly at Meg for the last time.

"Have no fear, for this will cost you no more than your agreement and a smidgeon of gratitude, for gratitude and thankfulness are worth more than a king's ransom."

The black vehicle pulled up silently beside the pair and a man got out. The Devil offered him a curt nod and he immediately began collecting all of Meg's things together before placing them into the boot of the car.

"Well, Meg, this is where I am obliged to take my leave of you, for I have others to see this night. You will be in safe hands with my colleague here, so do not fear."

Meg took hold of the Devil's hand and gripped it tightly.

"I don't understand," she said. "None of it makes any sense. What do you get out of this? I am very confused. And who are you?"

Taking hold of the handle of the vehicle door, the Devil opened it and ushered Meg inside.

"Let's say I get satisfaction out of a job well done," he answered. "And as to who I am – one of life's philanthropists I suppose."

Closing the car door, the vehicle slowly pulled away, leaving the Devil alone once more.

Chapter Three
The Third of the Dispossessed
The Professor

The Devil watched the vehicle somewhat pensively as it slowly disappeared into the night and then paused for a moment. He knew that Meg wasn't destined to live for very much longer. This was assured. Every living thing only ever had a certain amount of time allotted to them. And she was old and worn out and had a terminal illness that even she was unaware of. It was the culmination of years of sleeping rough that had put paid to any thought of a long and happy retirement. He knew that she would never return to this place, regardless of what he had promised her. But at least he was content in the knowledge that he had made her last few months on earth happy ones. It wasn't in his authority to bestow more life, regardless of the circumstances. Knowing he could have done no more, he turned on his heel and made his way back to Villiers Street.

As he stepped out into the road, he quickly crossed the street and made his way down towards Victoria Embankment Gardens. On his way, he passed two small takeaway establishments and a wine bar that appeared to be doing a very brisk trade, (which was hardly surprising for the time of year). Revellers were making the most of the time they had before they were all obliged to return home again. Everywhere was alive with activity. It positively thronged.

At last, he arrived at his destination: Victoria Embankment Gardens had existed in its present form for over one hundred years. It was a place that was normally open to the public during the day, whereby those who worked in the local offices and surrounding areas might use its facilities, usually to sit and take in its splendour and just for a short period of time escape from the pressures and rigours of city life. Large iron gates either end were locked at night, purely as a deterrent against precisely those sorts of people the Devil currently sought out. It was hard to imagine that a hundred plus years ago a river flowed here that fed into the Thames. It was a place where locals socialised, swam and made merry. It wasn't so very different now, minus the swimming of course.

As he stood before the large wrought iron gates, the Devil stopped and mulled over his next meeting. Engagements like this were never easy and they always required a resolute and sensitive manner. It was the only way they could ever work. Pursing his lips thoughtfully, he touched the large steel padlock that securely held the chain on the gates and watched as it fell away. Gently pushing the gate open, he entered.

The sight within that met his gaze was nothing less than spectacular – a veritable winter wonderland in fact. Snow covered everywhere and ran the whole length of the usually verdant oasis, unbroken, unmolested and un-trodden, due to the total absence of people that day; it stood out as a beacon of purity and glowed in an almost supernatural radiance against the evening gloom.

Slowly, he made his way towards the centre, picking his way carefully, until at last he encountered a very large yew tree. Still carrying its deep green needles, it looked altogether anomalous and out of place compared with all the other trees that now stood bare against the winter's eve. It was an old, gnarled tree, its lower branches hung low, forming a large canopy that might offer the disaffected and the homeless a retreat of some kind, but one of the starkest kind.

Knowing precisely where he had to go, the Devil pressed forward, bending the branches as he went. A deep wracking cough could be heard issuing forth from the tree's dim, dark and shadowy interior.

"Professor!" called the Devil in a hushed voice. "Are you there?"

The response was immediate and was one of panic.

"Who's there? Who is it?" came a male voice, quickly followed by another bout of coughing.

"You have nothing to fear," announced the Devil. "I am a friend. You may trust me."

An indistinct light suddenly came on, given off by a small pocket torch. The brightness it gave was feeble and insufficient for the space within and was swallowed up by the surrounding darkness. With a wave of his hand, the Devil made the tree's interior suddenly light up; a warm ambient effulgence spread out and seemed to dispel both darkness and cold simultaneously. It revealed sitting atop an old sleeping bag and a pile of newspapers, an elderly man. His aged rheumy eyes, viewing so little now, glared with fear and suspicion at this interloper.

"Who are you and what do you want? I'm not doing any harm here!" he voiced. The admission was little more than a severe cry for help, which the Devil was only too willing to acknowledge.

"Do not fear. I am an old student of yours, Professor," he said trying assure the old man as best he could. "I have to admit, it was many years ago now. More than I care to remember if I was honest. I studied under you at Pretherall College. Of course, you won't remember me after all this time, then why would you?"

The professor stifled another fit of coughing with an old handkerchief, which he pressed forcibly against his mouth. Flecks of old blood could be seen adhering to the cloth.

"Pretherall?" he finally announced through many distant recollections. "Yes, Pretherall… I taught there many years ago…I remember now… Who did you say you were again?"

"My name is Nicholas, but you wouldn't remember me. It has been so many years."

The elderly man looked on, his features wracked with age and ill health. His eyes screwed tightly as though trying to remember something from long, long ago.

"What did I teach you? My memory isn't what it was," he asked.

The Devil moved further in towards the old man's sanctum and found somewhere he was able to make himself relatively comfortable. The old man had covered most of the branches with black plastic bags in an attempt to block out the icy cold wind that assailed his tiny earthly abode. It had to be said his attempts had all but been in vain. However, with the

Devil's intervention, the interior now felt snug and warm and the old man was looking visibly the better for it.

"Theology and Comparative Religions mainly," replied the Devil at length. "And the meaning of life, of course."

The old man began to laugh quietly, before becoming overwhelmed by more fitful coughing.

"The meaning of life?" he echoed bitterly. "A little ironic, don't you think? As you can see this is hardly what you could consider the meaning of life, I mean. I think it may be true to say that I have aspired to very little that could be considered meaningful in my life – and I have achieved even less. With regards to the meaning of life, well let us say, I am still looking for it. I probably owe you an apology for wasting your early years for you. But there we have it. Nothing can be done now. How did you know I would be here of all places anyway? It is somewhat out of the way and I believe the gates are locked at six o'clock sharp. Did you scale the fence at all?"

"No," returned the Devil. "I didn't find the gates secured. Perhaps due to the time of year someone overlooked it. It's easily done."

"Yes, perhaps," replied the old man. "And as to how you knew I would be here?"

The Devil gave the semblance of giving the question much thought before offering his reply.

"I believe it was a former student who let it slip one lunch time. A while ago now. You see I don't work far from here. It may have been over a lunch time drink and conversation, something like that. To be honest, I don't remember. Anyhow, I was in the area and thought to see if there was any truth in the rumour."

The old man adjusted his position slightly and tried better to focus closer on his companion.

"Well, as you can see, your informant was correct. Here I reside for my pains, old, destitute, chronic lung disease and I'm dying. Probably won't last the night. A pretty good way to spend Christmas."

He began to cough once more. The Devil watched him with close scrutiny. The man's smallest movements quite clearly gave him great pain. It was apparent that what the man said was true. Death was very close now. In fact, it was no more than twenty minutes distant, although he didn't know that. But the Devil certainly did. He knew the precise moment it would happen. Time, it had to be said, was now of the essence.

"As you know I wasn't always as you see me now," said the old man. "Not when I was formally engaged in tutoring at Pretherall. Things didn't quite turn out as I might have hoped or expected. A bit of a downturn in fortune I'm afraid."

"Yes, I am only too aware of that," replied the Devil sympathetically. "Would you care to confide in me about it?"

The old man appeared to collect his scattered and worn-out thoughts before continuing.

"It was a long time ago now, so very long. I always regarded myself as a good mentor and tutor; I was always fair in my assessments. I endeavoured to help whenever possible... Always fair. I was always fair."

He fell away into a reverie of painful and unwanted memories.

The Devil pressed him gently to continue with his narrative and the old man eventually did so.

"It began when one day a student came to me about an essay I had set the whole class, said she couldn't fully comprehend what I was getting at, asked for additional help. A simple request – but like a fool I gave it – like a fool I gave no thought to the possible ramifications, the consequences. Needless to say, I was wrong – wrong about so many things."

He became thoughtful once again, lapsing into a dream like state. The Devil waited patiently for him to begin, being only too aware of the old man's story, but knowing that to admit as much would not have helped his cause. At last, the professor took up the story once more.

"The time came to inform them all of the marks that had been allocated for each piece of work. It had to be said that hers in particular was not good, despite my help and advice: it was ill thought out, rushed and lacked any substance. Substandard at best. I was obliged to give the work a D. To have done anything else would have been a betrayal of everything I knew. Naturally, she was not pleased with the result.

She asked for it to be re-marked. I said that was out of the question, as if I did it would mean I would merely be obliged to give it the same mark as before. It was at that point things began to turn rather unpleasant. You see I was then given an ultimatum. She told me in no uncertain terms that if I didn't review her work and improve the mark, I had given it, then she would lodge a complaint with the Dean, inferring that I had made improper suggestions and advances towards her. Naturally, if she had done that then my career would have been ruined, in tatters. Once besmirched in that way your reputation never recovers. Even had I stood my ground and told the truth, there would always have been rumours, sly innuendo, people forever talking discretely behind their hands, smirking as people are won't to do. It isn't something you get over. I agonised over what I should do for days, until I eventually did as she asked. I couldn't bear the shame and indignity of such a scandal. I would have been ruined. Her final mark was shown as a B, and believe me when I say it didn't warrant it."

"How did it make you feel?" the Devil asked.

"You may well imagine," replied the professor. "It sickened me to think that I had so little back bone, that I had so little courage and integrity. I was utterly ashamed, I had become hollow. I tried to console myself with the knowledge that in a year or so she would be gone, and that would be the end to it, that she would be nothing more than a bad memory. But I couldn't. Something inside of me felt betrayed, broken even. No matter what I did I couldn't seem to shake it from my soul. It was like an albatross around my neck, forever present, tangible and fetid. I sickened myself to the very core of my being by what I had done. The pain was unbearable. The only way I could deaden it was by drinking – and so I drank – and I drank – and I drank. It doesn't take much effort to see where it eventually led me. I lost my position and eventually everything else that was dear to me. Had I but the courage of my convictions back then, well, perhaps things may have been different. Who knows? But it is too late now."

He was subject to another coughing fit and pressed the battered unwashed kerchief against his mouth. When he had done the fresh blood upon it was only too apparent. In that moment, a large proportion of his life appeared to suddenly slip away, a bitter testament to a wasted and ruined life.

For a moment or so, they lapsed into silence once again. The old man was showing obvious signs that his life was in the process of ebbing away. Knowing how little time remained, the Devil pressed him.

"A sad tale, my friend," he remarked kindly. "But let us not dwell on such ugliness, not with the festive season upon us. I would like to ask you something if I may." The old man opened his eyes feebly and waited for the Devil to continue.

"Professor, if you could have the answer to any one question, be it anything at all, tell me what would it be?" he asked.

Turning slightly, the old man caught the Devil's eye and could see the sincerity in it.

"Oh, now there's a question. And that's a pretty tall order," he said. "Why do you ask such a thing? Are you going to tell me that you could supply the answer, regardless of what I might ask?"

"Yes. Precisely that," replied the Devil sounding very forthright. His riposte brooked no question that he could indeed supply the answer to anything the professor might ask.

"Well, I suppose if I had the opportunity to have any question answered truthfully then it would have to be 'What is the meaning of life and everything around us'."

"Then let me try and answer that question for you to the best of my ability. But to do that I need to show you something first." Here he helped the aged man carefully to his feet. Very slowly they emerged from the tree's canopy. The Devil placed a strong arm about the man's shoulders and supported him as if he weighed no more than a feather. Pointing up to the night sky, he then asked.

"Who made it, Professor? Everything in its entirety I mean?"

The question at first appeared to throw the old man. He wondered if this was an attempt to ridicule him; though for some reason, and he didn't know why, he doubted that. He chose to reply.

"Why God. God made it," he said.

"If you seriously believe that, then you are wrong in your assumption my friend, very wrong indeed," returned the Devil. "Let me do my utmost to explain why."

They made their way carefully back to the tree's warm interior and the old man was made as comfortable as the conditions would allow before the Devil continued with his explanation.

"Not wishing to disillusion you, Professor, but God had nothing to do with the creation of the universe – or anything else you see in front of your face – and that applies to the furthest corners of the cosmos – you see it was all your own doing."

The old man riled, naturally so.

"What?! Utter poppycock! Errant nonsense!" he growled and, in the process, sparked off another coughing fit.

"I will endeavour to make it plainer for you," said the Devil. "In the beginning, there was God and God chose to create Man in his own image. Not men I hasten to add, just Man, singular. And this is precisely what happened. This creation of God's is what is commonly known as Christ. So God created Christ and Christ had the power to create as did his father. Although God had created Christ, and they were one, there was total unity and only oneness. Then, for the briefest, smallest briefest fraction of time Christ wondered

47

what it would be like to be separate from its creator. And in that one tiniest speck, everything changed. God's creation fell into sleep and the seeming universe was created as it dreamed. God's creation dreamt and what passes for seeming reality was born. Everything you see around you from the closest flower to the furthest star is no more than an illusion. And in sleep everyone is seemingly born, a never-ending cycle of rebirth, but it is a reincarnation of the mind and not of the body. Whilst we all carry the subconscious guilt from that first moment of apparent separation, we continue reincarnating in sleep. It is the unconscious guilt each and every one carries in their mind which weighs us down like an anchor. That guilt is projected outwards and symbolically takes the form of everything you see – or at least you think you see. In reality, there is nothing out there. Nothing at all. It is an illusion of the grandest kind. Each and every one of us takes part in the same illusion, we merely see a different facet of it. You sleep, as does everyone else, waiting for the time when you will reawaken in heaven. True knowledge breaks the cycle and enables you to wake up and in order to get off the continuous merry-go-round of birth and death you must forgive everything that you believe you see before you. Forgiveness is the key. Never make what you believe you see before you real – for it is not. If we had more time, I would naturally explain to you in greater detail, but our time is unfortunately short and will not allow it. But you know of what I speak, don't you, my friend?"

The elderly man slowly lay back upon his bundle. A look of intense thoughtfulness crossed his face.

"Yes, I know. I've known for some time. A bit of a dishonourable end, don't you think? There's much to think about, so much, but so little time."

"The truth will always set you free. Forgive, do not hold on to your burden, for it is an illusion. Be at peace. Rest now," replied the Devil and took the old man's hand.

"The truth will set you free," echoed the old man as he closed his eyes for the final time. The Devil looked on in silence and waited. Within a few moments, the old man's breathing became shallow and then finally it stopped altogether. Rising, the Devil patted his hand gently and then turned and took his leave.

As he encountered the large metal gates from which had first entered the gardens, he stopped briefly upon exiting. Taking a small sign from his pocket he proceeded to attach it firmly to the iron railings. It read: *'There is an elderly gentleman within who passed away this Christmas Eve. Be so good as to deal with his remains kindly'.*

Chapter Four
The Fourth, Fifth and Sixth of
the Dispossessed Ed,
Barry and Razors

The snow had finally stopped falling as the Devil made his way down the remainder of Villiers Street and on to the Embankment. Despite the snowy respite, a severe northerly wind had now gotten up, whipping the fallen flakes into a series of frenetic dancing whorls that would have parodied a demonic display of the highest order. The Devil paid them no heed; he would soon be having an unwelcome meeting that would demand all of his attention and, what is more, test him to the limit.

Crossing Victoria Embankment, he stopped suddenly, his gaze taken by the sight of a young Asian woman sitting alone on a bench just a few yards from where he stood. He considered her situation. It all looked, he thought, rather incongruous, especially being Christmas Eve and all. Raising an eyebrow in curious contemplation, he consulted his pocket watch. As long as he didn't dawdle, he calculated that he just had sufficient time. Without a second thought, he made his way to where the young woman was sitting. Not wishing to alarm her unduly, he bent forward and retrieved a small bag from off the floor, which it had to be said had not been there a few seconds earlier.

"Excuse me," he said in the friendliest of tones, "but you appear to have dropped this."

The young woman, who had been deep in thought and had failed to notice him, looked up and seemed most surprised that the bag had managed to elude her grip and had somehow managed to fall to floor, especially when she was convinced that it had been wrapped around her arm when she initially sat down.

"Oh, thank you," she said taking the bag and examining it briefly. The strap seemed intact. How strange.

The Devil could see that the young woman was of Chinese origin and appeared to have something disturbing her. In normal circumstances, he wouldn't have bothered to have allowed himself to get side-tracked in this way, but something told him he just might be of assistance. And it always paid to enquire he found.

"Do you very much mind my asking," he said, "but is everything all right with you, only it seems altogether strange that a young woman, such as yourself, would be out so late in the evening and all alone too – and on Christmas Eve of all days of the year. Most odd, I thought. Shouldn't you be out celebrating with friends, or something like that?"

The young woman smiled in return.

"Yes, you might think that," she returned. "Christmas is something I don't usually celebrate. Even though I can appreciate all the festivities and everything that goes with it.

It's certainly a beautiful time of the year. And I know it's probably not prudent being out alone at this time of night, and especially in this weather, but I had to get out for a while and give myself some time to think. It's just been one of those days I'm afraid. Things just got a little on top of me. I just needed some fresh air, but I'm fine honestly, I really am. But thanks for asking."

She wasn't sure exactly why she found it so easy to confide in a perfect stranger. Normally, such an act would have been anathema to her. It really didn't make a lot of sense. There was no rationale to it, no sound reason or logic to it at all. But there it was. For some reason, she knew that the man offered no threat, though she couldn't have said why.

"Family getting a bit too much?" he offered by way of an introduction.

The young woman shook her head.

"Oh no, not at all. Nothing could be further from the truth. The answer to that question is a little more prosaic to be honest. You see I'm a writer and I'm currently working on a fairly big project. I have a deadline to meet and it's looming ever closer. Getting too close for comfort if the truth be told. Quite scary actually. There's lots of pressure. Too much in fact. I've reached a bit of an impasse with my writing and I'm not really sure how to get around it. I just needed some quiet time in which to think; clear my head a little and collect my thoughts, which is why you find me sitting on this bench in the snow on Christmas Eve. Odd really, I know. It must look utterly bizarre. But it works for me. Sometimes I just need to get out and be alone."

The Devil nodded in tacit agreement.

"Yes, funnily enough, I can relate all too well to that. I am often subject to writers block myself. I have to say it's never fun when it strikes. It drives me to the point of distraction if I was honest."

"You're a writer too?" she asked in surprise.

"Well, I suppose so; a writer of sorts anyway," replied the Devil. "Bit of a hack really. Writer? It's debatable if I was honest. I write magazine articles and periodicals from time to time. Nothing major, you understand. It's just bits and pieces. But it doesn't matter what you turn out, ultimately you still need the old neurons to keep on firing in the old head, or it doesn't work, don't you know?"

She laughed loudly, finding him amusing and altogether good company. A kindred spirit in fact. And she rarely met any of those in her line of work.

"Yes, I know precisely what you mean," she said. "It's great when it just flows. There's no greater feeling than when inspiration takes a hold. The writing just seems to go on and on. It's wonderful. I love it."

"Exactly. I really couldn't agree more. I'm Nick by the way," he said and extended a hand in warm greeting. The young woman took his hand and shook it.

"My friends call me Shez," she said and smiled warmly.

"Well it's a pleasure to make your acquaintance," he said. "Do you mind very much if I sit down for a moment? I am supposed to be meeting three colleagues here very soon now. We have a lot to discuss, but I have a bit of time to kill, and to be honest with you my feet are killing me in these shoes. They're brand new you see. I thought I would wear them in a bit, but now I'm beginning to think that was a bit of a mistake."

"No, feel free. To be honest, I was just about to return home. I've been sitting here for over an hour already and my thoughts are beginning to gel again. I think it's all finally coming together at long last. Sometimes you just need to sit it out for a while. But I'm fine now. It's amazing what the cold night air can achieve at times. Though I wouldn't usually recommend it on nights like this. It's pretty cold."

"Well, I'm very glad to hear it. That's really excellent news!" said the Devil brightly and promptly sat down on the bench next to her.

"Do you enjoy writing?" she asked him. "The actual process I mean. I have to say I sometimes find it a bit of a drudge. I seem to have lost the initial pleasure I got from it and I'm not sure why that is so. I often wonder if maybe I'm not cut out for it."

"Yes, that does happen from time to time," he replied. "But I still love it, nevertheless. And I think that there's no better way of earning a living, not when the inspiration is in full flow, as you have already pointed out. Though if I'm honest I do it mainly for the sheer hell of it nowadays. I don't have to write at all to be perfectly frank with you, as I have private means. I do it, in the main, because something drives me to do it; and I will continue to do so until the day arrives when I tire of it fully. And may God bless it, that's what I say."

Shez applauded.

"Here here," she said and then added. "I hope you don't mind my asking, but did you say you were carrying out business? I mean, here, now, on Christmas Eve of all nights? Only you said you were meeting your colleagues here soon.

It just strikes me as a bit of a peculiar thing to do." She seemed most perplexed at the very notion of it.

The Devil shook his head wearily, nodded and sighed.

"Well, it's business of a sort," he remarked sadly. "Let's say it's more of an attempt at redemption more than anything else. I find it always pays to give everyone the chance to put things right. To give them the benefit of the doubt so to speak. Few of them rarely do in my experience. Such are the ways of life. It's a terrible waste really, but there we are. I don't make the rules. I merely implement them."

"Redemption? Wow, these guys must have done something pretty bad!" she exclaimed. "I can't even begin to imagine what it must be."

The Devil agreed.

"Yes, they have, and unless I can prevent it, they will continue to do so again and again and so on ad infinitum. I think it would to true to say that they are now currently caught between the Devil and the deep blue sea. And that is not a good place to be. Time is definitely running out for them – as it invariably does for everyone. It is inexorable you see. It is a never-ending cycle." He laughed, though in truth it sounded more like a wordless exclamation than anything else. "Well, I regret to say that I must leave you now. I have thoroughly enjoyed our little chat. Oh and before I go, a short word of advice; don't give any further thought to dead-lines and the accompanying pressure that goes with it. Once it all gets to be a drudge, then it's time to call a halt to it. My recommendation is to enjoy it. Nothing more. Merely enjoy it. If you do that it will become a lot easier and you will get a lot more out of it. Never lose sight of why you started this in the first place, to do so is to allow yourself to fall into the pit of regret. It's never worth it. Trust me."

Rising from the bench, he wished her well and also the compliments of the season. The young woman also rose.

"Thank you," she said with a smile. "I shall take your advice, as it makes a lot of sense. Funnily enough, I used to enjoy it far more than I do now. Not sure where it all went wrong really."

"And you will again – trust me in this," he said.

He watched her go, albeit with a feeling of fulfilment and joy. Did she but know that in a very short space of time she would become well known for her writings. Famous in fact. It had to said that life never ceased to amaze him.

"It just needs a little faith," he muttered to himself. "And now for the task in hand. Heaven help me."

Picking his way amongst the mounds of ice and snow that littered the pavement, he crossed the road and made his way to the Thames River wall. Placing his hands upon its lintel, he gazed out across the river's dark sombre waters. The remorseless wind continued whipping the waves into a frenzy. As he looked out across the river, he reflected upon times gone by. A kaleidoscope of images, both old and new, began to coalesce before his eyes. The new: The London Eye. Very popular by all accounts, but not something that stirred his emotions greatly. Far too modern. It didn't really seem to fit in with its surroundings. Somewhat anomalous. Each to their own as they say. And the old: Seeing St Paul's Cathedral in all its glory, having usurped the original in the fiery conflagration that took place hundreds of years before. He'd been there at the time and witnessed it all: the Black Death, the Great Fire. They were troubled times indeed. No, not good at all. Things had improved immeasurably since those days, but oddly enough people were just the same. There was good and bad in everyone, and of course the same was to be said for most things. The trick was to encourage the good and then watch it flourish.

It was at that precise moment, lost in his thoughts that he was, he detected the nearby sound of those whose reason it was for him being there. It was in the guise of three young men who were fast approaching.

"Evil under the sun," he mumbled beneath his breath and proceeded to wait patiently. Slowly, he began to count quietly to himself. "Ten – nine – eight – seven – six – five – four – three – two," and finally, "one."

It was time.

"Hey mate, you got a light?" came a voice. It was a rough and uncouth voice. Any sign of manners were made very obvious by their absence.

Turning, the Devil saw before him a triad of life's foulest human flotsam. Three young men, unkempt, unwashed and riddled through and through with the after-effects of drink and drugs. They were thin, hollow men, bereft of compassion or love and without any redeeming features whatsoever. They had become victims of their own neglect and apathy to life and everything wholesome thing it stood for; festering in what passed for life and with no apparent desire to change.

"Christmas felicitations to you gentleman one and all!" he said in an overwhelming gesture of sincere friendliness. "I trust you are all well?"

The three seemed overwhelmed, not knowing quite how to respond to this greeting. None of the three chose to speak. They merely looked on, staring, vacuous, puzzled and unsure.

Then, the leader, grunted once again, "I said, you got a light mate?"

The Devil looked deep into the man's eyes, viewing the shrivelled state of what passed for his soul, which had been the culmination of constant years of self-neglect, abuse and a staunch unwillingness to change. Evil ways fitted him like a glove. The man was apparently bereft of virtually any capacity for good, despite the last vestigial spark of the divine that slumbered deep within him. But, despite this, the Devil chose to give all three the benefit of the doubt. That was his job.

"Yes, of course I do," he finally announced and produced a lighter from his coat pocket. The man took it without offering any sign of gratitude.

"So, you're Ed, are you?" the Devil asked merrily.

The man's sunken eyes suddenly blazed with a ferocious intensity.

"How do you know my name?" he asked sharply. "I don't know you."

Pointing to the front of the man's jacket, the Devil, forever maintaining his good humour throughout, replied, "The name Ed is emblazoned upon the front of your jacket there. I assume therefore that it must be yours. Is that not so?"

Ed cooled, grudgingly admitting that it was his name.

"Er – yeah," he uttered.

"And who are your friends here?" continued the Devil.

"Er…Barry and Razors," replied Ed after a moment.

Raising his eyebrows, the Devil asked.

"Razors? Well, that's an unusual name, isn't it? And how may I ask did you obtain such a curious appellation?"

"Appe…what?" returned a very confused Razors.

The Devil smiled broadly, but with no hint at condescension.

"Your name – Razors. I merely wondered how you came by it," he said.

Razors grinned. It was an evil grin, full of malevolence and coldness. He removed a long-bladed knife from his pocket.

"Why, well it's cos I cut things," he said without any sign of emotion. "Razors – see?"

"Cut things, eh? I do see. Well, we don't want you cutting anything on Christmas Eve, do we?" said the Devil with great emphasis. "Cutting things, I mean. That would never do. Terrible state of affairs."

The three men looked at one another and looked on in a particularly malicious and unified fashion. They were as one. Ed then spoke for them all.

"Well now, that really depends, doesn't it?" he said, grinning once again, revealing a mouthful of rotten teeth in the process.

"Does it?" asked the Devil innocently. "Upon what does it depend, if you don't mind my asking?"

Ed then produced a long thin bladed knife of his own. Both men proceeded to point them belligerently towards him. The Devil gave the semblance of being shocked by their actions.

"It depends upon wevver or not you have any money on you, or some other valuables, such as watches, credit cards, things like that – we ain't fussy," announced Ed. "And it also depends upon wevver you choose to turn 'em over to us. Being Christmas like. It's charitable, innit?"

The Devil feigned much innocence.

"Regrettably, I have to say cash is something I have little need of in my line of work," he replied truthfully. "If I was honest with you, I have to say I have none at all. Not so much as a sou, a bean or a farthing. I am so sorry."

It was apparent that none of the men believed him.

"Is that so?" said Ed and pushed the blade still further in the direction of the Devil's coat, brushing it this way and that over the material in an attempt to intimidate and frighten. If that was his intention, it had to be said it was wasted on his victim.

"If I may be so bold and offer some advice in the form of a very old saying to you gentlemen," said the Devil cordially, "and that is 'He who sups with the Devil should use a very long spoon'. Now, you may call me naïve if you will, and if you did then that would be a blunder of the greatest magnitude on your part, but I really don't for one moment believe that any of you gentlemen has a spoon anywhere near long enough for the task in hand."

"What's he fackin talkin' about?" growled Razors aggressively and approached the Devil with his knife held high.

"I dunno," replied Ed. "But I do know that unless our friend here hands over his wallet and anything else of value, and he's pretty quick about it then we're gonna slice him up six ways till Saturday. Which will real spoil his Christmas. Well, pal, what's it to be? It's your choice."

Quickly removing a leather wallet from his inside coat pocket, the Devil handed it over to Ed, who then proceeded to roughly go through it.

"It's fuckin empty!" he howled. "There's shit all in it!" Throwing it angrily to the floor, he grabbed the lapel of the

Devil's coat and tugged it roughly. "We ain't messin' about here, friend! Now, you either hand over any cash, cards or valuables that you have on you or you're brown bread. Do you understand? Is that clear? And that means DEAD! D-E-A-D! Got it?"

The Devil nodded, his eyes now imperceptibly narrowing for the second time that evening.

"Oh I can assure you that I understand, Edward. You may believe me when I say I understand you better than you can even begin to imagine. Let me give you one final piece of advice; and once again this is given in the spirit in which it is intended and you would be well advised to take it, for I sincerely believe that the Devil should always be given his due: and that piece of advice is 'If you keep knocking on the Devil's door, then sooner or later he will invariably let you in'. And believe me when I say that is something you really do not want to experience. Believe me. I now strongly advise you all to dwell on that for a moment or two otherwise you may do something you will all later sincerely regret."

"He's off his bleeding chump, is this one!" barked Barry. "Let's do for him and get out of here before someone comes along!"

Ed nodded in agreement.

"I'm all for that." Turning to the Devil, he asked, "Well, what's it to be chummy? You gonna hand over what you've got in your pockets or do me and the lads here cut you up? Nice way to spend Christmas. Your choice, fella."

Pursing his lips, as if deep in thought, the Devil looked from one to the other. Nowhere amongst them did he discern any sign of remorse or any wish to refrain from their intended course. It genuinely saddened him. He felt as he had failed in his task. And it angered him. It angered him mightily.

"My friends! May I appeal to you one last time, not only because of the festive time of year, a time when men generally unlock their frozen hearts and endeavour to show a modicum of good will to others, but also because not one of you fully understand the implications and ramifications of what you are getting yourselves into. Pull back from the abyss and repent – while there is still time. There is no shame in it."

"I've had enough of this bullshit!" shouted Razer's and plunged his blade deep into the Devil's coat.

The Devil, un-phased and unmoved by the action, sighed loudly and shook his head in obvious disappointment. Their time had finally come.

"Oh dear, oh dear, oh dear," he said. "That, my friend, was the final deed that sealed all of your fates. You had a choice. I gave it to you more than once. And now you have finally committed that one sin that showed that you have at last 'crossed the Rubicon' as it were. There is no going back for you now."

Ed, Barry and Razer's looked on bemused and horrified by what they had just witnessed. The Devil should be bleeding profusely by now, lying prostrate in the snow, breathing his last, but clearly, he wasn't. Something was definitely amiss. Ed plunged his own knife into the Devil and felt the razor-sharp blade enter his body. It met no resistance at all, as if passing through empty air. Once again, their victim was unmoved by the action and merely continued standing there smiling.

"What are you?" he asked stepping back, altogether bewildered and perplexed.

Adjusting his coat, which now showed no signs of being penetrated by either blade, the Devil answered, "If you drop the interrogative and reverse your question, you will then have your answer." Seeing that none of them had any idea as to what he was talking about, he proceeded to explain. "Lose the What, reverse the 'are you' and your question then becomes a statement: 'You are' and indeed I very much am. Well gentlemen, enough of this tomfoolery and time-consuming badinage. It is time, I believe, for a slight reversal of fortune. I would greatly appreciate it if you would all deposit your weaponry in the river you see before you. And please be quick about it."

Showing neither the ability nor the will to refuse the command, all three walked calmly to the river wall and threw their knives into the Thames. They suddenly seemed without resolve or purpose and not one of them could fully comprehend why. The Devil then continued.

"Strange, is it not, don't you think, that should I wish to do so I can kill a man where he stands, with no more than a thought; I can rain brimstone and fire down upon his head when it suits me to do so, but even I cannot change a man's mind. I cannot change that which intrinsically makes him what he his. And yet I do not judge anyone, least of all yourselves – you each and every one of you do this to yourselves by the very action of your thoughts, deeds and actions; and that is what constantly saddens me. And I genuinely pray for the day when it doesn't. But now, my friends, having disposed of your arms, if you would please be so good, it is time for the three of you to follow suit."

Ed, Barry and Razors had been standing stock still up until this point, in a near comatose state, taking in everything that the Devil had said to them. They found that they had as much ability to oppose his will as they had to make the sun come out and shine down upon them at that particular moment. One by one the three men slowly climbed the wall in a zombie like manner and went the same way as their knives. The initial splash was punctuated by a brief silence, only to be followed by a second and finally a third. In less than ten seconds the Devil stood alone once more looking out upon the river which had consumed them.

Moving purposefully to the wall, at the very spot where the three men had consigned themselves to their dark watery graves just seconds earlier, he peered into the depths below.

"Do not fret, my friends," he murmured. "We shall be seeing one another very soon. You have much to learn and your training starts now."

Having finalised his business, he turned at last and re-crossed Victoria Embankment. As he did so, he encountered a small group of Christmas revellers. They approached him, on their way either home, or to meet up with other likeminded party goers out for a good time. They wished him glad tidings and the warmth of the season. Bowing low, the Devil did the same and then repeated the sentiments – and what's more, he meant it.

Chapter Five
The Seventh of the
Dispossessed May

Before continuing his evening vigil, he stopped for the last time and gazed wistfully out along the river. He wouldn't see it again for some time and he wanted to make the most of this opportunity. Many was the time over the years when he had done this and it had always given him such joy; buildings of grand design having come and gone down the years. The ever-changing face of the old girl. An image of the original London bridge came to mind and it made him smile. The splendid old city had changed much down the centuries. He remembered fondly when the last icy snap had frozen the river solid. Yes, the Thames. Hard to believe now. What a year that had been. Eighteen fourteen to be exact. Yes, that was it. A long time ago, but still very memorable none-the-less. He seemed to recall that such was the very coldness of the year and the frozen nature of the river, someone had thought it amusing to take an elephant out onto it. They did, and the ice surprisingly held up. *Crazy times,* he thought. It made him smile.

The same church clock from earlier now struck the half hour. He consulted his pocket watch again. The clock's chimes peeled stridently, as if urging him on to endeavours anew. He listened attentively, nodded and then went on his way. Proceeding up Northumberland Avenue, he passed the Playhouse Theatre and then moved on into Craven Street. All was deathly quiet around this part of the city, it being a place given over to offices and very little else. Taking a sharp right, he entered a small thoroughfare that passed behind the shops and the buildings. The light here was subdued, having little or no function during the evening hours. With a purpose the Devil marched on until he came to a narrow access between two buildings; so insignificant was this ingress it was easy to pass during the day, which made spotting it even more difficult during the dark hours. The silence here had become near corporeal; though nothing at all stirred within. Having no desire to frighten his next assignation, he waited momentarily before softly calling her name: "May," he said. At first there was no response, all was quiet. He had fully expected this. Then he called again, slightly louder this time. An indistinct shuffling of sorts could then be heard emanating from the depths of the passageway, though still nothing could be seen through the murk. The sound slowly got closer, then it stopped altogether. Whatever had made it was now staying well back out of sight, unsure and cautious. The Devil persisted, knowing that this was not going to be easy, and he called for a third time.

"May! Please, I mean you no harm," he delivered soothingly. "I am here to help you. Won't you speak with me a moment?"

A thoughtful silence ensued, almost as if the person in the recess was giving the matter much thought. After a brief spell, a young querulous female voice called out. "Who's there? Who is it?"

The Devil immediately called back.

"May, have no fear, I am a friend. I have been looking for you for some time. I am here to help. You can trust me."

Another short silence followed. There was more rustling. Eventually, a young girl emerged from the shadows. She must have been no older than sixteen at the very most and she looked absolutely terrified. Around her shoulders, she wore a blanket, which she now pulled tightly about herself to ward off the intense cold. It was a thin, ragged blanket and was full of holes – it was nothing against such bitter freezing weather as this.

"Hello, May," said the Devil. "My name's Nick. I'm a private detective. I know this probably sounds utterly crazy, but your parents have asked me to find you. I've been trying to track you down for days, and now I've finally got lucky. Oh and before I forget, I was asked to let you have these. I think you may find them useful, especially in this cold weather."

Producing a padded thermal coat, gloves, scarf and hat from beneath his arm, he handed them across to her. Despite her uncertainty she was only too glad to accept them and quickly put them on. Very soon, she was benefiting from the welcome gifts.

"How did you know to find me here?" she asked tremulously, finding it all rather strange that anyone could have discovered where she was. It was all too obvious that the girl was utterly terrified.

The Devil went on to explain.

"No great mystery really," he said. "It was all down to lots of hard work, talking to lots of people, making sure I showed your picture to anyone and everyone I met, including all the homeless people in the vicinity; all in the vain hope that something would turn up. To be honest over the past few days I have tried looking everywhere I could think of. I knew I was getting close when I spoke to a young man earlier today. I can't remember his name – not that it's important – but he did say he had seen you once or twice recently in the vicinity. Then it was really just a case of plugging away until I found you. And here I am."

May looked at him intensely, trying to find some reason not to trust him, but try as she might, she couldn't.

"Are you sure they want me to come home? I mean did they really say that? I don't think they do," she said, sounding very unsure.

The Devil looked upon her kindly and smiled reassuringly and even in the dismal light she appeared to sense his goodwill and benevolence.

"Well, May, that's not what they told me. And just think about it for a moment. Why would they go to all the trouble and the expense of hiring me unless they truly did want you to come home? It has to be said, my fees aren't exactly cheap. And believe me, on Christmas Eve I charge significantly more for my labours."

What the private detective said made a lot of sense to her. Why would her parents go to all this trouble and expense unless they really wanted her to come home again? But even so, she still wasn't fully convinced, and it showed in her face.

"Ah, I see I haven't fully won you over with my story. And that's to be understood, May. You are bound to still have doubts. That's perfectly natural. Here, may be this will this help to persuade you. It's my ID and a letter from your parents, instructing me to find you." He handed them both over to her. In the murky light she tried to read them, but couldn't as the light was too bad. "It's a trifle dark. Here try this." He took out a small torch and handed it across to her. May used its light to view the documents. Eventually, she appeared satisfied and handed them back to him.

"That's my mom's writing. I recognised it straight away," she said, sounding a little more relieved.

The Devil seemed most pleased that she at last was willing to give him the benefit of the doubt.

"Look, I don't know about you but I'm freezing to death standing here," he said. "I know of a great place just near the Charing Cross Road. It's still open and it sells the most delicious hot chocolate. I know I could do with warming up, and I feel sure that you could as well. Why don't we have a slow walk over there and I will answer whatever questions you might have? How does that sound?"

The prospect did not seem to fill May with the sort of assurance she needed in order to trust this man. Her scepticism was written across her features for all to see. Although he had produced apparent ID, confirming who he was and also his purpose, and not forgetting of course the letter from her mother, there was something altogether strangely unnerving about him; something, if she was forced to state precisely what it was, she could not have done so. All she knew was she didn't wholly trust him. And now he was asking her to accompany him. Weighing up her situation, she figured if it became necessary then she could probably outrun him (especially in those shoes he was wearing). She figured that if she kept sufficient distance between the two of them then she should be fine. So that is what she chose to do.

The Devil, for his part, had little trouble reading her thoughts and her intentions. He was after all rather good at it. Her reluctance didn't faze him one bit. Why should it? No one trusts the Devil and that was to be expected. *It was his lot in life. C'est le vie,* he thought to himself and then proceeded to put the next phase of his plan into action.

Taking a small set of panpipes from inside his coat pocket, he placed them against his lips and gently began to blow. May stopped and watched what he was doing. She was puzzled, though not alarmed. It just seemed so very odd to her that he would be playing a musical instrument at this time of night in the middle of London, and in these conditions to boot. Was the man mad after all?

Initially, the music began slowly; it was mellow and rather comforting in its way, but then it started to build, getting louder and louder and ever faster. The notes appeared to fly straight from the panpipes with a frenetic energy, taking on an almost magical visible outline as they flew, soared, dipped and generally filled the air and all their surroundings with a supernatural vibrancy that lit up and invigorated the whole place. Everything outside of their unnatural musical enclosure appeared to stop. The whole world had stopped. There was now nothing else. All that existed was the music. Despite herself, May could feel her feet beginning to move in time to it. She couldn't help herself – what's more she didn't want to help herself – all there was now was the music and she was compelled to follow it no matter where it led. And had she been honest, she didn't care one bit. No, not one iota. On and on, it played. The buildings and all her surroundings coalesced and merged into one giant phantasmagoria of wall-to-wall magical sound. She danced, she skipped, she pirouetted – she moved – all in perfect synchronicity and in harmony with the notes. It felt invigorating and she felt alive.

Then suddenly and without warning it stopped, as magically as it had begun. All that was left was the Devil standing there in the street sporting a very large grin. May felt both exhilarated and exhausted. Never before had she experienced anything like it. It was magical.

"What was that?" she asked breathlessly.

The Devil gave her a sly wink.

"A small composition of my own making. Do you feel any better?" he asked mischievously.

And in truth, she did feel better – a whole lot better in fact, better than she had felt in a very long time.

"Yes, yes I do," she heard herself say. The admission caused her some embarrassment and she felt herself blushing, and was thankful of the gloom to hide the redness of her cheeks.

"Let's go and get some hot chocolate," he announced, quickly replacing the panpipes from whence they had come. "The weather is beginning to deteriorate once again and time is waning fast – and there is still much to do. So very much to do."

Increasing his pace, the Devil moved on, with May following on closely behind. There were few people about now, as most had either returned home or were on their way home. Christmas Day was not far off, beckoning, forever beckoning and bed was the only thing on most people's minds.

Crossing the Strand, the pair walked the short distance to the Charing Cross Road and the Devil immediately headed for a small café that still appeared to be open.

"Nothing like a cup of steaming hot chocolate to keep out the cold," he announced merrily and plunged straight through the door. Quickly ordering up two large mugs of chocolate-delight, he and May then sat by the window and watched as the snow began to come down again, even heavier than before. Removing his gloves, the Devil raised a hand to the café owner and proceeded to order up a large chocolate muffin to go with the chocolate.

"Thought it might come in handy," he said, "considering. And the chocolate muffins they sell here are exceptional. I have no doubt you are probably feeling a tad hungry." Admitted that she was. In fact, she felt ravenous.

"I had some soup earlier," she admitted. "Though I've had nothing since then."

The Devil scrutinised her closely, his eyes though kind pierced her through to the deepest recesses of her soul.

"Well," he declared after a moment. "Perhaps you would kindly fill me in with the details about why you left home – how long has it been now?"

The question made her feel uncomfortable, causing her to avert her gaze. She began to fiddle nervously with the paper napkin in front of her and look for things out of the window.

"It's been two weeks," she eventually confessed. "Or about that, I think. It seems longer though, a lot longer."

"I'm not at all surprised," said the Devil. "Time has the objectionable knack of stretching itself out when things aren't

72

going well. Have you been sleeping rough ever since you left home?"

She said that initially she had spent the first few days at a friend's house. Then it turned out not to be convenient for her to remain any longer, so she was asked to leave.

"I've only been sleeping rough for a few days," she confessed. "It isn't nice. It's been very cold. Most of the time, you are so cold you can't sleep at all. I don't like it. I get scared a lot. And people usually aren't very kind when they know that you are homeless."

The Devil nodded sympathetically.

"Yes, being homeless and cold is not anything any of us would ever wish for. It's a positively wretched state of affairs at best. May I ask, what was your initial reason for leaving home? I mean, it must have been pretty bad."

"It was something very silly," she reluctantly acknowledged. "I had a falling out with my stepdad. Nothing serious. Stupid really."

"Oh, did you indeed? Nothing serious, eh? Well, I feel that it must have been a pretty bad falling out for you to give up a nice warm home and a loving family, and then trade it all in for a life on the streets. I have to say, when I initially met your family, I thought your mom seemed kind, but I have to say that I wasn't overly taken with your step-father. Call it a gut reaction if you will. I had a bad feeling right from the outset. In my line of work, you get an innate ability to weigh people up pretty quickly, you see their true nature. And it's usually very accurate—"

"But it wasn't like that," May objected, knowing that her stepfather was in fact a rather kindly man. At that moment, the café owner arrived with two steaming mugs of hot chocolate and a very large chocolate muffin. The Devil waited for him to leave before continuing.

"I bet he treated you really badly, as I can usually tell. Did he beat you at all? I have to admit, he looks the sort that might. The thought of it makes my blood boil I can tell you. I have a loathing for bullies. I tell you something, the very next time I see him I guarantee I will—"

May rose heatedly from her seat. She had become most agitated listening to the Devil berating her stepfather.

"But I tell you it wasn't like that!" she yelled. "We just had a falling out. That's all there was too it. Please leave it."

The Devil gently sipped at his hot chocolate, allowing a moment or two to calm down. He then asked her.

"You're not just saying that I hope, because if I thought for one second that he had hurt you in any way, I promise I would make him regret it until the day he died. Nothing worse than a tyrant in my estimation! All you need to do is to say the word and I—"

At this point, May began to get very animated once more, waving her arms about in obvious frustration at the man's obvious inability to listen to what she had to say.

"Look, he told me off for not helping my mom about the house when he was out at work. We had an argument about it and I walked out. That's it! That's all there is! There's nothing else!"

She sat down again, looking both angry and frustrated.

Having finally exposed the truth, she sat staring into her drink rather solemnly. The Devil raised an eyebrow, and then a second.

"I see," he said pointedly. "And there was me thinking that nothing short of hell had broken loose in your home, and that was the reason you left. And yet all this time it was something as irrelevant and inconsequential as that. Well – well – well. My – oh – my. Who would have thought it, I ask? All this upset and heartache simply because you wouldn't tidy your room? How very odd. How very very odd. So, let me get this perfectly clear, in effect it was partly your own fault?"

May nodded without looking him in the eye.

"Yes," she admitted reluctantly. "Yes, I suppose it was."

"Well, on the basis of what you have just told me, I would have to say that it sounds very much, in fact, like the majority of it was all your fault, and not your stepfather's at all," continued the Devil professing surprise as he said it.

All May could do in response was to nod in agreement and continue to stare into her hot chocolate.

"Well, I have to say, I feel that admission puts a whole different reflection on things. If it was something so trivial as that then why haven't you returned home before now?" he asked. "That would have been the common-sense thing to do, don't you think?"

May sighed.

"I wanted to, I really wanted to. I thought about it a lot, especially over the last few days, and especially when it began to get really cold. The more I thought about it the more I thought that maybe they didn't want me back. Not after the falling out. I did try, but I just couldn't make myself do it. It was impossible."

The Devil nodded in understanding.

"It would seem that you were wrong about that as well," he said in a slightly admonishing way. May had to agree.

"Yes, I suppose so," she replied.

"An apology might, I think, be in order," he pressed. "And a pretty big one at that, especially considering the trouble and the heartache you have caused – and not forgetting the exorbitant cost – and all this just before Christmas time too. A valuable lesson there I believe and no mistake."

May wiped a tear away from her eye with her sleeve and slowly sipped her hot chocolate.

"I know. It was my fault, and I should say sorry to them."

"Well, that's good to hear," he said smiling kindly. "And you should get the opportunity to do just that very soon, for if I'm not mistaken, your mom and dad has just pulled up outside."

"What? My mom!" May said shocked by the news. Getting to her feet, she quickly looked around to see if it was true.

"Yes, May. You see, thinking that this might be the outcome, I took the trouble of ringing your parents over an hour ago and asked them to meet us here. Bit of a liberty I suppose, considering I had no real idea as to the possible outcome of all this, but I always say nothing ventured nothing gained etc., etc., eh?"

May rushed excitedly to the door, opened it quickly and began to look out through the heavily falling snow, scouring left and right for any sign of her parents.

"You say my mom an' dad's here! But I can't see them!"

The Devil rose from his chair and slowly replaced his gloves.

"Be patient, May. They may be a little way up the street looking for somewhere to park. If you pop out now, you should see them."

May didn't need telling twice, she hurried out into the drifting snow. She could see that true to his word her mother and stepfather had pulled up just a short distance along the street. Her mother jumped out of the car and the two ran to one another and embraced, a fierce embrace. Tears flowed on all sides. After a few moments, when all the emotions at last had time to settle, May's mother announced, "I genuinely thought that phone call we received earlier from the police was a hoax. I really never expected to see you here! I can't believe it."

Through a barrage of tears and pent-up emotion, May finally managed to blurt out, "That would have been from the Private detective. He's not a policeman, but he seems very nice. He said that he rang you about an hour ago to let you know."

Her mother looked puzzled by this announcement.

"What do you mean, Private detective?" she asked. "What Private detective?"

It was now May's turn to appear puzzled.

"The one you sent to look for me," she replied. "He rang you. About an hour ago. He said so. Though he must have rung you before he found me and I have no idea how he managed to do that. Come and ask him yourself. We were having hot chocolate when you arrived, in this café here—" May stopped, shocked by what she now saw before her. The café, where only minutes before she had been seated enjoying a hot beverage with the Devil, was now no longer visible. It was gone. In its place, there stood a stationery shop. Having no lights on, it was definitely closed for the Christmas period. May shook her head and began pacing back and forth along the street, utterly bemused as to how anything of this nature could possibly have happened. There was no way she could have made such an error. She had only come a few yards. It should be here. It had to be here. Where had it gone?

Her mother and stepfather exchanged glances and then finally took her gently by the shoulders and escorted her back to the waiting car. They would try and get to the bottom of all this confusion once they safely had her home again. No doubt she was confused due to her traumatic experience. It was inevitable.

As the car slowly pulled away, the Devil, from the other side of the street, casually watched it go. He smiled a self-satisfied smile.

Chapter Six
The Eighth, Ninth and Tenth of the Dispossessed Laz, Dominic and Lucy

The snow continued falling, more heavily now than it had done at any time that evening, blanketing central London for as far as the eye could see in a thick brilliant white covering. The brightness of the Christmas lights reflected warmly from its surface, which gave everything a tender glow and a deceptive appearance of warmth. But nothing could have been further from the truth. The thermometer had dropped alarmingly, meaning there would be many who would fail to make it through the long hours this night. The Devil shook his head sadly. How easy it would be to change the order of things. If everyone simply chose to change for the good. But he knew that was not ever going to happen. The script didn't call for it. And that particular piece of knowledge did not fill him with joy, as you might well expect. Well, there was little or no point standing here pontificating and gathering snow, he thought to himself. There's still work to be done.

Briskly, he set off, once again returning to Craven Street, the same place he had located May just a short time earlier. There were other fish to fry there, and this particular encounter was not going to provide him with any Christmas cheer, of that he was absolutely convinced.

Approximately half way down the street, he stopped at a large Georgian building. It was an imposing edifice and stood three stories high. Attached to the railings that adorned its front was a large estate agent's sign. It advertised 'Office Space to Let'. He knew that the building had been empty for many months, but despite that it still had residents occupied within. It was those residents that he now targeted.

Mounting the series of steps that ran to the large white painted front door, he stopped. Everywhere was locked up tightly. This of course had not failed to deter the present incumbents that currently resided inside. They had originally gained access through the rear, by forcing a window and had been happily ensconced here for the best part of two months. As the place was not alarmed, entry had proven relatively easy.

Taking hold of the large brass knob, he turned it slowly. Being able to gain access to any house, room, building or domicile was one of the perks of the job, and one that always gave him a certain child-like Devilish thrill. If he was honest with himself, this time was one of those episodes when it did not. Having the ability to foresee what was ahead may have its obvious intrinsic appeal, but there were times, such as now, when he wished otherwise. Never mind, he thought, needs must when the Devil drives and all that. And so, he ploughed on.

Pushing the door slightly ajar, he entered the building, closing it quietly after him. He had no desire to alert those within to his presence, at least not yet. If he did then he knew they could always use what time they had to scuttle out of the back and his visit would have been in vain. The sizeable hallway was, dark, cold and altogether depressing, there now being no light to reflect its former opulence. Moving forward, he ascended the stairs two at a time until he reached the first floor. He knew the room he was looking for lay at the rear of the property. This particular room had been chosen carefully by those who were now squatting here in order to mask their occupancy from any prying eyes. The door he was looking for lay at the end of a short corridor. Listening intently, he could hear no sounds issuing forth from those within, there was only a ruddy light that could be seen escaping from beneath the door.

Well, here goes nothing, he thought and taking the handle firmly and with purpose he turned it and entered the room. It turned out to be a large office space, though was now devoid of any furniture. At the far end was an old black grate where a small fire was burning. Some of the floorboards had been prised up, no doubt to provide kindling for the fire. To the right of the fireplace, there lay a rather grubby mattress, upon which there rested lengthways a young man. He didn't move and looked rather pale and listless. He was also frighteningly thin. His features were drawn and ashen and there appeared little life in him, and what remained was undoubtedly feeble, throttled and pathetic. Sitting at the end of the mattress was a young woman of tender years. She was propped up against the wall with her head bowed and her dark sunken eyes firmly closed. There was little sign of life in her, but the spark that still remained was no more than a smouldering remnant of what it used to be and what it ought to be. It was obvious that they were both on drugs of one sort or another. The Devil watched them both closely for a moment, thinking what a sad waste of human existence it was. Neither of these two young people were aware of his presence. To see the magnificence of life in all its potential and spiritual wonder debased in such a way as this was almost beyond his will to bear. He considered the irony that went with this scene, a scene he had observed over and over again, an irony that was never ever lost on him. Whenever something like this occurred, he invariably got the blame for it: 'It's the Devil's doing!' he would hear, or 'They've got the Devil in them', was how it usually went more often than not. Well, that was the way of things. That was life. He found it just paid you to get on with things and keep your head down wherever possible.

As he continued to observe the two, the young woman appeared to at last sense someone's presence. Opening her eyes, she stared at the Devil briefly and then asked through a haze of drug induced feebleness.

"W… Who are you?"

The Devil smiled.

"I am Father Christmas – come a little early," he announced quietly. "Not that you would necessarily recognise me in my current get-up. Still being in the early stages of youth, my beard and hair have yet to turn white and I left my suit in the sleigh. But that aside, I still come bearing gifts and good cheer."

Through the mental fog she was currently experiencing, the young woman tried to take on board precisely what he had said. It all seemed too confusing to her. Having had many similar episodes previously, due to the effects of the drugs, most of which rarely made any sense, she closed her eyes again briefly, knowing that as soon as she opened them once more the man, whoever or whatever he was, would undoubtedly be gone. She did and he wasn't.

"Are you r…real?" she asked weakly, doing her utmost to focus on him. "Or are you in my head? I see things – things."

Moving more central, so that she could get a better look at him, the Devil replied, "I have to say that there's little or no difference if I was honest with you. And you wouldn't understand it if I explained it to you. Let's say I am real for now. Did you say that your name was Lucy?"

"Did I? I can't remember. Yes, I suppose I did. That's my name. Yes, Lucy."

"And this is your friend Dominic?"

The girl nodded and moved her hand protectively towards him.

The girl looked vague.

"Dominic," she uttered instinctively.

"I get no pleasure from having to tell you this, Lucy, but your friend Dominic here is very unwell. He needs to be in a hospital. If he doesn't get medical help, and get it soon, then he will die. You have to take my word for that. You need to let me help him."

Lucy moved unconsciously towards the young man, who lay so still and inert upon the mattress he could well have been a corpse.

"He's fine here with me," she stated protectively, placing herself as best she could between the young man and the Devil. "I look after him. I've always looked after him. All he needs is a little rest and he'll be fine."

The Devil took a small step forward, though not too far, as he did not wish to alarm her greatly.

"No, he won't, Lucy. I don't wish to contradict you, but you are very wrong on this point. Already he lies between life and death, and unless we get him to some proper medical care, then it will be too late. I can arrange to give him the help and care he requires, if you will just let me."

At this point, the girl became very disturbed, blocking any access to the young man on the bed with her physical presence, of which it had to be said there was very little.

"We don't need your help!" she cried. "Go away and leave us alone! You aren't real – I know you're not real! – You're in my head! Go away! Just go away!"

The Devil shook his head sadly, knowing it would come to this regardless of what he said or did. He moved still closer, fully aware that time was now running out.

"No, Lucy, I cannot do that. Your friend Dominic is clearly dying. He desperately needs my help, and he needs it sooner rather than later. You must let me help."

Instinctively, Lucy reached out for whatever came to hand, for a way of protecting them both. She took hold of an old newspaper and a magazine from the bed and threw it at him. Needless to say, it had little effect.

"Get out of here! You're not real! You're just in my head! You're the Devil – that's what you are! You're the Devil, and you're in my head!"

The Devil nodded in acquiescence.

"Who I am has little or no relevance at this precise moment. And being the Devil doesn't make my intentions any less honourable or compassionate. Your friend here needs help, there's very little else I can say. He must have it and so must you."

"Oh, is that right?" came a voice from behind him. "And who might you be?"

The Devil turned to see a tall, angular looking young man. He was carrying a small crowbar and had a load of broken floor boards beneath his arm. It looked as if he had obviously been very busy.

"Ah, you must be Laz I presume?" said the Devil. "Been stocking up on firewood I see? I have little doubt the estate agent responsible for this block is going to ultimately find out that most of the rooms here will now not have the wherewithal to support anyone in the immediate future, at least not after your exploits with that little tyre iron of yours. Would I be correct in that assumption?"

Dropping the wood on to the floor, Laz raised the crowbar and advanced on the Devil, who stood irresolute and unflinching.

"Who the fuck are you?" he demanded, waving the bar from side to side. "You a copper or something?"

The Devil's eyebrows rose slightly.

"Copper, as in the curious cockney colloquialism for a member of the constabulary? No, sorry to disappoint you there, Laz. I must say, you have such a way with you do you not? Now I would ask you to kindly put that crowbar down before someone gets very badly hurt. And of the two of us, believe me when I say I know which one of us it is likely to be."

The advice, though well intentioned, fell on deaf ears. Laz advanced threateningly.

"How about you cut the mouth and tell us who you are and how you managed to get in here? That front door is locked securely, and the back one is bolted from the inside, so unless you're a magician I suggest you start giving us a few answers, or I'll split your head open like an over-ripe melon."

The Devil indicated the young man lying on the bed.

"As much as I would dearly like to spend the rest of the night having a discourse with you on the merits of breaking and entering without a key, Laz, I regret to say that your friend here cannot spare the time. So, for the nonce, I think it is in his interests to get him some help. Wouldn't you agree?"

"And I say he don't need any help. He's better off here where I can keep an eye on him. And what's it to do with you anyway? You his bleeding father or something? Now answer my question before I take this to your skull and ruin your Christmas for good – how did you get in here?"

The Devil sighed deeply. People could often be so irascible and predictable at times. It was so tedious.

"I would like to appeal to your sense of humanity for the very last time, Laz, that is if you have any in you. Would you kindly allow me to help your colleague here before it is too late? I implore you."

Once again, the Devil's plea fell upon deaf ears which, in all truth, he knew it probably would. There was only one course of action now that Laz would understand. Having looked deep within the man's soul, he knew that any petition on his part would merely be met with intransigence, loathing and possible violence. The man was without a doubt beyond redemption. The Devil pulled a large wad of rolled banknotes from his pocket and then made a great show of waving them beneath Laz's nose. The effect it had upon him was like magic. A smile began to spread across the young man's face, a near lascivious lust born of pure greed. At once, the crowbar was consigned to the floor, only to be replaced by an unctuous Laz, only too happy to comply.

"Why didn't you say so? Now you're talking my language. I gets your drift, man. I mean, there's no point in losing your rag at Christmas time now, is there? You can do whatever you like with him as far as I'm concerned. He's only cluttering up the place anyway."

"He is indeed, Laz, he is indeed," returned the Devil. "I have three friends currently waiting for me down by the Embankment. They are known as Ed, Barry and Razors. They are currently feeling a little low and could do with some festive stimulation, if you get my meaning, (here he winked knowingly) a small pick me up, yes? Now, if you could see your way clear to taking this money and perhaps going and seeing my friends and offer them a little Christmas cheer. Oh, and tell them that I will be along very soon."

Laz grabbed the money that was offered greedily and then quickly disappeared, leaving the Devil alone with Lucy and Dominic. Beneath his breath, the Devil muttered, "The wretch, concentred all in self, living, shall forfeit fair renown, and doubly dying, shall go down to the vile dust from whence he sprung, unwept, un-honoured and unsung. And a very good riddance."

Lucy looked up at him, unsure of what to either say or do. Now that Laz had gone, she felt hesitant and even more uncertain about things. In an attempt to put her at her ease, the Devil spoke with great compassion.

"Don't be alarmed, Lucy. As I said, Dominic here urgently needs our help. I have a private ambulance waiting just outside in the street. The paramedics will treat you both well. I have made sure of that. Go with them now. They know what they have to do."

Without a further word being said, the door opened and two orderlies silently entered; they were carrying a stretcher. Lucy watched as they gently took hold of Dominic and placed him upon it."

Where will they take him?" she asked.

"To a local hospital of my choosing," answered the Devil. "I need you to accompany him for me and see that he gets well again. Look after him, as he needs you now probably more so than he has ever done. The staff will look after you. That much I promise."

"Aren't you are coming with us?" she asked, but the Devil only shook his head.

"As much as I would like to, I have to say, regrettably, I cannot. There is still much for me to do this night and time moves on remorselessly. Tempus fugit as the old saying goes. Time flies."

Lucy began to make her way to the door, then stopped.

"What about Laz?" she asked.

The Devil smiled broadly and replied.

"Have no fear about him, Lucy. I can give you my heartfelt assurance that I shall be looking out for him personally. He has been well and truly factored into my plans."

Smiling, albeit a mite timidly, Lucy followed the two orderlies out of the room. Once alone, the Devil took out his pocket watch and glanced at it.

"Oh my," he said with some alarm. "Time does indeed move on. I must be off."

Leaving the building at a brisk pace, he quickly headed in the direction of the Strand, moving perhaps a mite quicker than he would normally have done.

Chapter Seven
The Eleventh of the
Dispossessed Miriam

As he crossed Trafalgar Square, the Devil suddenly stopped, took out his pocket watch and consulted it once again. The time showed 10.37. A trifle late to go calling on people he thought. But it couldn't be helped. Things rarely went according to how you wanted them to. That was the nature of the beast.

Increasing his pace, he entered Cockspur Street and immediately made for a small office block. Avoiding the front of the building, he made his way around to the rear and stopped at an ornate, metal fire escape. Instead of going up, he chose the stairs that led inexorably down. He soon found himself confronted by a large grey metal door.

"Well, I suppose I had better be well prepared," he said to himself, and in the blink of an eye he sported a pair of thick, heavy spectacles; a briefcase also appeared in his left hand. With the other hand, he smote heavily upon the metal door and then listened to the faint echoes as they reverberated within. Initially, there was no response. Which was hardly surprising given the circumstances and the time of night.

Then, within a moment or two, a muffled female voice could be heard from the other side of the metal door.

"Who is it?" it called.

The Devil put on his most gracious voice and then called back.

"Hello. Is that Miriam, Miriam Barcley?"

"Er…Ye…es. Who are you? And what do you want?" the voice called back. This was accompanied by the sound of a dog barking ferociously.

"My name is Siddlestone," called the Devil – Henry Siddlestone. I represent Langton, Merriwether and Filllimont, solicitors at Law. I shall pop my card beneath the door for you to see."

He duly did so. There was a short cessation, where neither female nor dog could be heard. Then the woman called out.

"What do you want? It's late."

Raising his eyebrows in quiet frustration, the Devil maintained his good humour and replied:

"It would be a lot easier to talk with you face to face Miriam. I have to say the weather out here is particularly inclement and the snow seems to be gathering apace. Not nice at all, and not at all conducive to carrying out a conversation through a metal door. Could you kindly spare me a few moments of your time, so that I may explain? I can't overestimate the importance of my visit here this evening. And you will no doubt appreciate that my being here must endorse that."

Again, there was a short silence. This was followed by the sound of a large bolt being thrown, then another. The door opened slightly, but not sufficient enough to let him inside.

"I have a dog. He doesn't take to strangers," she informed him. "He's very protective of me."

The Devil continued to remain amiable.

"Yes, I could distinctly make him out," he said, doing his level best to remain agreeable. "I have little doubt he offers you good protection at all times. May I please come in?"

The woman, who must have been in her sixties, was thin, angular and dressed in what appeared to be a man's greatcoat. This stretched from her neck to her feet. She also sported a large brown woolly hat and a thick muffler. The whole ensemble was topped off by a pair of thick woolly purple mittens.

"I can take care of myself," she offered. "Me and Tigger here. We don't stand any messing from anyone. I warn you."

The Devil smiled and nodded in complete agreement and understanding.

"No, I bet you don't. Well, you can't afford to be too careful nowadays, can you? So many undesirables about. It's not a good world at the best of times. It's difficult to know who you can trust. Now, if I could just come in for a moment. I promise I won't keep you any longer than is necessary. I can see that you're busy and I don't wish to intrude any longer than I have to."

Miriam moved to one side to allow him access. The dog, which was a large burly, well-muscled, Staffordshire Bull terrier came up to him and wagged its tail profusely, obviously only too happy to welcome their uninvited visitor irrespective of the time of day.

"Well, that's odd," she Miriam. "Old Tigger normally don't take to men. Never has. They're not to be trusted you see – men. I was just going to bed."

The Devil nodded affably and smiled.

"Yes, yes, I can see that. Sorry to catch you in your night attire. I wouldn't normally call at this time of day, especially on such a night of the year as this; however, it has taken me quite some time to track you down and I didn't want to let this golden opportunity pass me by, Christmas Eve or not."

As they moved further into, what appeared to be a corridor, the Devil could see that at one end was a strange construction made from what appeared to be an enormous cardboard box. It was big enough to have contained a fridge freezer at one time – and a pretty large one at that. It had been lined with what appeared to be thick industrial foam. As odd as it all appeared, it also gave the impression of being very comfortable and warm. Miriam could see him observing it closely. She smiled proudly.

"Not exactly the Dorchester, I know," she said, "but once we are inside with the flap closed, it gets more than warm enough for me and Tigger here. Sleep like babies we do."

"Yes, yes I bet you do. It looks really nice and cosy. A very sought-after des-res, or so I believe the expression goes."

Miriam looked him up and down.

"Do you work here or something?" she asked. "If you do, then we aren't doing any harm. We look after the place when no one's here. Old Joe said it was okay to stay. They never come down here anyway, them people upstairs. It's the basement. There's nothing down here. I don't know why they have to get a lawyer to come and throw me out of my home on Christmas Eve. We've haven't done anything wrong. I've got nowhere else to go. Me and Tigger will freeze to death."

The Devil moved further down the corridor and found a small packing case in which to place his briefcase.

"No, no, please don't get unduly upset, Miriam. I have nothing at all to do with this particular organisation. You may take my word for that. I am merely a solicitor, not a lawyer. My purpose here is purely business and not the least also one of compassion. As I said just now, I represent the law firm Langton, Merriwether and Filllimont, as stated on the card. We have been endeavouring to locate you for some time now, er – I assume it is all right to call you Miriam – good, that's excellent. Is there anywhere where I may sit briefly, only I have one or two things to impart to you and standing up for any length of time invariably causes me cramp?"

Miriam found two small wooden boxes upon which to sit.

"I'm a bit confused as to how you managed to find me, down here I mean," she said. "I didn't think anyone knew about us, Tigger and me."

"Well, your friend Joe the caretaker here certainly does," replied the Devil. "All it took was a bit of detective work on our part. Quite academic really. You'd be surprised at the proficiency of the network we have built up in the city over the years. Very little goes by without it being brought to our attention. But that isn't really important at this precise moment. What is significant is that I have managed to locate you, so if we could get down to business and I will tell you the reason why I am here."

He sat down upon one of the boxes and Miriam did the same. At this juncture, the Devil opened his briefcase and removed a cardboard folder from it."

"I have here certain documents here that I need you to look at, if you would be so good," he said.

"Documents? What sort of documents?" she asked guardedly.

"Well, you see, we, that is Langton, Merriwether and Filllimont, represented your late husband in an official capacity," he explained.

"Late? You say – Late? Is the old bugger finally dead then?" she asked, without showing any sign of remorse.

"Well, yes, I'm afraid to say that that does appear to be the case. I believe he passed away about a month ago now. I am very sorry to be the harbinger of bad news like this. It is never easy, I know."

Miriam got to her feet and straight away began to dance a little jig, much to the Devil's surprise.

"Bad news, did you say? Bad news? That's got to be the best Christmas present you could have brought me!" she exclaimed and did another jig.

Feigning surprise and not the least astonishment, the Devil asked her.

"I take it you that you didn't get along too well then?"

Miriam stopped her cavorting and looked him squarely in the eye.

"Didn't get along too well?" she echoed. "Too damn right we didn't get along too well. It's because of that sod I'm homeless! You may take it from me Mr – whatever your name is, when I say I loathed the old bugger with a passion! He was a tyrant and a monster to live with, and I put up with it for over twenty years. He never had a kind word for me in all that time, even though I washed and cooked and cleaned for him. It was a constant nightmare! I hated him, and now you come and tell me he's dead, and I tell you that I'm glad about it. You can bet the old bugger is now in hell, roasting away with all the other buggers. And I tell you this, it's no less than he deserves. I'm glad he's gone and that's that."

The Devil was genuinely taken aback by her vitriolic outburst, and it took a great deal to shock him. He bade her sit down, which she eventually did.

"I can assure you, Miriam that your deceased husband is not in hell. Trust me when I say I speak with authority on this matter. And despite the fact he may have treated you perhaps say we say, perhaps not as well as he should have during his lifetime, in death, I believe, we should give him a certain modicum of respect, don't you?"

At once, Miriam was on her feet again.

"He led me merry hell when I was married to him. It was worse than a dog's life – day after day after day. And if he's not burning in hell, then he should be. Best place for the old bleeder in my opinion. No one will shed a tear now he's gone – and you can take MY word for that. He lived his life as a pig and he died a pig – and I'm glad he's dead!"

Giving the intensity of her emotional flare-up, the Devil thought it better to endeavour to try and pour a little balm upon troubled waters.

"We each and every one of us often do and say things that in later life may cause us regret, things which we may repent about much later, and this is often the way. It allows us to consider others, what they may have been going through, their thoughts and their feelings. Ultimately, it is only in our own interests to let these feelings of negativity go. We should try and forgive, as to do otherwise means we then have a great burden to bear. And this burden has greater ramifications than we can possibly imagine at the time. My advice to you, Miriam, is to let go of your anger and hatred."

She was on her feet once again, belligerent and ready for a fight. Only this time, she began gesticulating wildly and pointing, at what can only be described as an admonishing finger at the Devil. He sat quietly on his upturned box and took it with the good grace you might not have expected from him.

"I can't let it go and I won't!" she howled. "You've got no right coming in here telling me what I can and cannot do, and whether or not I can hate my husband. You didn't have to put up with his temper and his drunken tantrums day in day out. It's all very easy sitting there sounding holier than thou, but I bet if push came to shove you wouldn't have put up with it not for a moment! I said I hated him and I do, and nothing you can say will change that for a minute. He's dead and I'm glad he's dead!"

Miriam stuck out her jaw, as if to emphasise her feelings and said, "I've said my piece and that's that, take it or leave it."

The Devil, therefore, chose to do the latter. He had come here with the sole intention of informing her, not only of her husband's unfortunate demise, but also that, as she was the only remaining heir to his estate, she would inherit everything he owned. But her hatred and intensity of mind, and unwillingness to show any form of compassion in the matter, had shown him she was simply not worthy of it. Slowly, he replaced the folder back into his briefcase. Then, rising he said, "Well, I've taken up enough of your time, Miriam. It's getting late and it's dropping even colder out there, so I must be off. Long way to go, don't you know? I wish you the compliments of the season and I urge you to stay safe, and naturally to keep warm if you can."

As he turned to go, a stunned Miriam called after him.

"Is that it then? I mean, is that all? You've come all this way just to tell me he's dead? Isn't there anything else?"

"What else would there be?" returned the Devil as he made his way to the door.

"Well, I don't know. Did he leave any money or anything? What about the house? Half of it was mine you know. I want what's coming to me!"

The Devil smiled as cordially as the situation would allow.

"Yes, I feel sure that you do, Miriam, and that's perfectly understandable. I suppose I should have mentioned it before. A bit remiss of me I know. I'm afraid your husband frittered it all away, every last penny. It looks as though a few months ago he took out a second mortgage on the house, and then lost it all on the gee-gees, or the dogs; something like that anyway. Not quite sure which it was to be honest. A very sad affair, I know that, and one that I am altogether bereft at having to come here on Christmas Eve and inform you about – however, that is the way the cookie crumbles – as the old saying goes."

A very shocked, and not to say the least disappointed, Miriam said, "So, there's nothing left? Nothing? Not a sausage? Nothing at all?"

"No, not so much as bean," answered the Devil dispassionately, and opening the door quickly let himself out into the snow. As he walked away, he heard the sound of the door behind him being slammed firmly shut. It was a slam that spoke volumes: of betrayal – disappointment – resentment – and hatred, being the most evident. But, as the Devil often said, that's life.

Chapter Eight
The Twelfth of the
Dispossessed Michael Asquith

Re-crossing Trafalgar Square for the second time that night, the Devil allowed himself all but a brief moment to take in Nelson's Column. People rarely looked at it nowadays, he thought to himself; rather like a favourite picture they have on a wall in their home for years but acknowledge only when they haven't done so in a while. What a pity, especially considering the statues magnificence. Erected in honour of the great man, few people actually realised that it had been carved from solid granite, thinking it more of a bronze effigy. In the past, parts of it had become damaged and bits had actually flaked off, resulting in repairs having to be made. Those charged with the task of carrying them out, had merely filled in the holes and the missing bits with good old cement. Not that you could tell from down here of course, he was too far off the ground to tell. It had always struck him as odd, that the statue, being granite, had been placed upon a bronze plinth;

making him wonder why they hadn't gone the whole hog when it had first been commissioned and simply made the whole thing from the same material. It would have made far more sense. He could only assume that at the time cost must have been an issue. Well, it had certainly cost the local authority a great deal more since; proving that penny pinching never pays in the long term.

He breathed in a lungful of the chill night air and took in the extremity of the vista before him. There were the two fountains and the six large lions in all their grandeur – utterly magnificent in their entirety. He could cast his mind back to long before any of this was here. Two hundred years before all this was stables – linked to the Horse Guards Parade just across the way there. *Everything changes,* he thought, *everything is in a constant state of flux.*

He was about to continue on his way, when his eye caught a young man sitting on the steps in the square. He was all alone, with nothing but an umbrella to keep off the ever-falling snow. How very odd, he thought. The man appeared well dressed, and not in need of any particular attention that he could see. It seemed to be a curious thing to be doing on Christmas Eve of all nights, all things considered that is. The Devil felt that ever present tingling he usually got when called upon to intervene. Either for good or ill, it always gave him a thrill. *Oh well*, he thought, *here goes nothing, yet again.* Once more unto the breach and all that.

As he slowly made his way across to where the young man was seated, the Devil's visage changed in an instant. Gone was the spring in the step, the vibrancy, the sleek black hair, only to be replaced by a grey beard, heavy facial lines and a walking cane – and not forgetting an umbrella to ward off the snow. The young man appeared thoroughly absorbed in his own misery and failed to see the older man walking in his direction with slow measured steps towards him. Feigning much discomfort, and a desperate need to take a break, the old man said, "Do you mind very much if I join you, only I need to rest my leg for a minute or two? It's giving me a bit of jip. An old wound."

The young man looked up distractedly from beneath his umbrella, his wretchedness etched into every part of his face.

"I'd prefer to be alone if you don't mind," he said coolly.

The old man chuckled.

"Yes, I'm sure you would Michael, but I'm afraid my old leg says otherwise. If I don't sit down soon, I'm afraid I am liable to fall down. And I feel sure that you wouldn't want that on your conscience now, would you?"

At the mention of his name, the young man, utterly shocked, looked up.

"Have we met before?" he asked.

The old man shook his head, a decidedly mischievous glint in his eye.

"No, no never; at least I don't think we have. Don't look too put out by my knowing your name. There's no mystery to it. It's engraved on your briefcase just there. See?"

He pointed to it with his cane. The young man instantly looked relieved.

"Oh, yes of course."

"Do you see that small round building over there?" continued the old man. "That odd one with the dome on it? Funny looking little thing it is. Can you see?"

"What about it?" Michael asked, beginning to believe that an old loner with nothing else better to do had attached himself to him. That was all he needed just now.

"Did you know that's the oldest police box in the whole of London. It's been there decades. Naturally, it isn't used for its original purpose anymore; no longer any need for it, not with the advent of mobile phones and walkie-talkies and the like. Still, it makes for an interesting snippet of information, don't you think?"

Michael nodded without showing any real interest.

"Yes, yes I suppose it is," he said.

The old man took out a plastic carrier bag and placed it upon the step next to Michael and then proceeded to sit on it.

"Oh, that's better. A bit of a weight off. Be all right in a few minutes. Just need to get the circulation going again and then I'll be on my way. I can see you need to be alone. Lots to think about no doubt?"

"Yes, something like that," replied Michael.

"Saying that though, I don't imagine that whatever it is that's bothering you can be that bad," said the old man as he rubbed his leg.

A very bemused Michael asked, "Why do you say that?"

"Oh, a simple observation. I'm a great observer of people. Always have been. I find it often pays big dividends. You never know when you can offer a piece of advice, even with the most trivial and mundane of problems. Always trying to help, that's me."

"I'm sure you are. But if it's all the same to you, I would prefer to keep my problems and their solutions to myself. Don't misunderstand me, I'm not trying to be rude, I just need time to think. That's why I chose this place. I didn't expect to be bothered."

The old man nodded in agreement, choosing to ignore the sarcasm.

"Well, that goes without saying. But even so, as I pointed out only a moment ago, it can't be that bad, whatever it is that's bothering you."

A rather irritated Michael asked tersely, "And what makes you say that? You have no idea what it is that's bothering me. How can you?"

The old man nodded.

"Well, to begin with, like me, you're sitting on a plastic bag to protect your coat. Now, if you were so deeply wrapped up with your problem (whatever that may be) then you wouldn't give a second thought to it now, would you? It stands to reason."

"No, perhaps not," answered Michael, rather half-heartedly. He really wished that this old man would take his observations and just leave him alone. "May be, like you, I just needed to rest awhile. Have you considered that?"

The old man laughed out loud. It was the sort of laugh Santa Claus might make, on this night of all nights, just prior to setting off on his sleigh happy in the knowledge of what was to come.

"Well, call me Mr Psychic if you will," he said maintaining his good humour. "But all you have to do is to look around and you will see that there is no truth in what you say at all. Don't take offence, as none was intended. I merely point out that it is Christmas Eve, people are moving about hither and thither – all of them with a profound purpose, either to make someone happy, or even if it just to make themselves happy – though usually it's others. And yet here you sit, all alone in the snow, looking both maudlin and morose, on the one night of the year when veritable magic fills the air. Peoples, hearts soar with the sheer knowledge of it being Christmas – and you're are all alone and with nothing apparently wrong with you. It doesn't take much working out, does it?"

The old man lapsed into a long silence, allowing Michael to ponder upon what he had said. He pondered over it for many minutes before eventually responding.

"Look, let's just say that my Christmas is going to be memorable for all the wrong reasons, and leave it at that, shall we? There's nothing further to add."

"It doesn't have to be memorable for all the wrong reasons," piped up the old man.

Michael was by now beginning to get a little heated, and he didn't give a hoot if the old man knew it.

"Oh yes, and how would you know?" he asked angrily. "You don't know me! You're just someone who happened to show up when I wasn't expecting it, nothing more. And believe me, when I say, it's nothing I need."

The old man leant in close, continuing with his beatific smile.

"Sometimes, seemingly chance encounters are brought about for the sole purpose of allowing us to resolve things we wouldn't ordinarily be able to resolve ourselves."

"Well, is that a fact?" returned Michael, his ire beginning to rise to the surface now. The old man nodded and smiled, apparently oblivious to it.

"Yes, call it fate, kismet or destiny, whatever you like – or maybe it is all three. Who can say? All I know is that you are a young man who thinks the weight of the whole world is currently pressing down upon his shoulders, when in fact it isn't. Not a bit of it."

"And how precisely would you know that? Are you genuinely psychic or something?"

The old man looked on kindly; there was no malice showing in his face.

"You'd be most surprised what I know about you, Michael," he replied.

There was something about the old man's tone, his mannerisms that told Michael that what he said was true, even though he didn't know the man at all, and also knew that he couldn't really know anything about him as they had never met before. So, just why exactly did it bother him so much?

"Go on then," he said, choosing to give the old man enough leeway to make a fool of himself, "enlighten me. You tell me exactly what it is you think you know about me and we'll both have a good laugh when you are wrong."

The old man made a great show of rubbing his chin through his long grey beard, whilst looking Michael up and down, as if gaining inspiration from it.

"Well, I can see you are, as they say, on the horns of a dilemma. A dilemma, I would say, that is of your own making. You smell of alcohol, (no offence) so it's not difficult to assume that you have been celebrating perhaps a little too richly throughout the evening. And yet you are now perfectly sober, as sober as a judge in fact; hence I have to assume that something altogether earth-shattering has happened in your life over the last hour or so to make you so. I also see residing next to you a small bag with the logo and name of one of London's most prestigious, and not to say expensive, jewellers on it. Carnelles of Bond Street, I believe. You are wearing a handmade Saville Row suit, diamond studded gold cufflinks and a very expensive watch – so it would appear that money is of no object to you. Now, what I know of that particular shop is that they tend to cater towards jewellery of a more intimate nature: such as rings, necklaces, earrings and things of that sort."

At this point, the old man took out his watch and consulted it.

"They will have been closed for many hours now, so the question I am forced to ask is, exactly where have you been hiding yourself for the last four and a half hours? Somewhere, I believe, that has caused you both great recrimination and not to say the least a very large helping of conscience, which is why you are apparently in the doldrums now. Marry all that together, along with the alcohol and everything becomes plain. Am I wrong?"

Michael sat up opened mouthed. Everything the old man had said was true. But how did he know? Was it purely guess work alone? He asked incredulously, "How do you know all this?"

"I thought I had just explained that to you at great length," replied the old man. "Anyhow, it's really pretty prosaic, no mystery at all, it is simply the application of deductive reasoning, as practised by none other than Mr Sherlock Holmes. That's where I have just come from by the way, The Sherlock Holmes pub. It's based just across the way there. Did you know, they have a room in there solely given over to 221B Baker Street. It looks just like how you might imagine his parlour to look. Amazing stuff. I'm a great fan of the old sleuth and his methods. Nearly always right. All you have to do is just follow the obvious. Sticks out like a sore thumb. Well?"

Michael was near speechless by what the old man had said. And it was a little too near the truth for comfort. It made him uncomfortable.

"Well, what?" he asked, shaking his head.

"Oh, Michael, you really don't need to be so obtuse. It doesn't fit you not for one moment. Was my interpretation of the facts correct?"

Michael reluctantly admitted that it was, which caused the old man to nod.

"So, you left work, bought the gift, then no doubt popped back to your place of work to meet with your colleagues for a celebratory drink? One thing led to another (which it invariably does where alcohol is concerned) then the indiscretion took place. And no doubt you have been sitting here ever since feeling very sorry for yourself. Is that correct?"

Michael agreed that it was.

"Yes, everything that you say is true. How can I go home now, knowing what I have done? I can't live with myself, which is why I have been sitting here all this time. I don't know how to deal with it."

"It certainly isn't easy I will grant you that. But what you have to do now is to weigh up the consequences and look for the best outcome."

"I'm not quite sure precisely what you mean. The consequences are obvious: I admit to my wrongdoing and that's it, finished. It's over. There's no going back. And I deserve it."

The old man placed a comforting hand upon Michael's shoulder and gave it a reassuring squeeze.

"Sometimes, telling someone the truth is the worst possible option. It is always important to look at the bigger picture. This will then enable you to do what is right, but not necessarily what is true."

Michael ran a hand across his brow in frustration.

"You're talking in riddles. What you are saying makes no sense at all."

The old man rose from the step upon which he had been sitting and leaned heavily upon his cane for support.

"Answer me this," he asked. "Exactly how much do you love her?"

"Love her?" echoed Michael. "Why more than anything, and this is why it hurts so much. I've been a fool and I know…"

"And what would it do to her to learn the truth?" interrupted the old man.

"It would destroy her, utterly destroy her," Michael admitted and put his head in his hands in despair.

"Then you must not tell her. This must be your burden and your burden alone. She has done nothing to deserve it. Use the pain you are experiencing to make her life a happy one, and also use it to ensure that you never make the same mistake twice. As I said, look for the bigger picture. Do what is right. Always do what is right."

For some time, Michael considered the old man's words, paroxysms of conscience and doubt creasing his features every now and then.

"I don't think I could keep it to myself," he said. "It isn't really an option for me. I just couldn't do it."

"You have no choice in the matter!" raged the old man. "This is your penance. Your punishment is your continuing silence, and it will live with you until the very day that you eventually learn to let it go and forgive yourself. And that day will come in time, but until it does each day that you live will feel forever as if you have been cursed. That is your fate – your sentence!"

Michael fell silent, taking in the full meaning and implications of what the old man had said to him. In his heart, he knew what he had heard was true.

"Do you really believe that this is my best option?" he asked at last. "It just doesn't seem right. It feels so wrong."

Patting his knee, the old man collected his plastic bag, upon which he had been sitting, and answered, "It is your only option, my boy. Take my word for it."

"But I deserve hell for what I've done!"

The old man laughed loudly.

"Believe me, Michael, hell is inhabited by people far worse than you. All you need to remember is to remain on the straight and narrow and you will be fine. The straight and narrow. Remember what I have said now and don't ever forget it. Now, I must be off. My leg is feeling a whole lot better for a rest."

Getting to his feet, Michael extended a hand in gratitude. The old man took it and shook it warmly.

"Thank you for your understanding and kind words. I don't deserve it. You can't even begin to imagine how much they have helped."

"Oh, I have a pretty good idea," returned the old man. "Now I think it time that you were getting along too. You've been gone long enough."

Turning to go, Michael paused briefly, collected his case and his gift and smiled. Then he was gone, swallowed up by the ever-falling snow.

The Devil turned up his collar on his astrakhan coat and set off across Trafalgar Square again, knowing that Michael, despite being on an emotional roller-coaster, would ultimately come good. He wouldn't find things easy, but then anything in life was always worth fighting for.

In the blink of an eye, there was no sign of his umbrella, his long grey beard, or his walking cane. As he was leaving the Square, he stopped suddenly and using his shoe, pushed aside the snow in a particular place. It revealed a small round piece of gold coloured metal that had been impressed into the pavement; something so non-descript you wouldn't have noticed it unless you was aware that it was there. Smiling, the Devil could be heard muttering, "That small piece of metal represents the very centre of London – and not many people are aware of that."

Giving a little skip, he went merrily on his way, humming a little Christmas ditty as he went. He just loved this time of year.

Chapter Nine
The Thirteenth of the
Dispossessed Rev. Adrian Noble

Just off the Charing Cross road, secretly tucked away behind the back of Bernier Street, there resides a small unostentatious church called St Luciens. It was built during the reign of Elizabeth the first. An unremarkable building in itself, not imposing and now nearly completely obscured by the other buildings that have encroached upon it down the centuries; enveloped, near submerged and almost forgotten. If you didn't know of its existence beforehand, then in all likelihood you never would. It's dwindling congregation had been matched only by its upkeep. In short, it looked and was, down at heel, being desperately in need of significant repair, plus a lot of tender loving care. The faithful few who continued to attend this rather sad little structure had, of recent months, been unable to do even that, owing to the repair work that was needed as a matter of great urgency. The church chancel required underpinning in order to render the building safe again. Once the extent of the repairs required had been determined, a fund was organised by the incumbent Reverend – a one Adrian Noble. Precisely six months later, the total raised had now amounted to a staggering three hundred and sixty-four pounds and twenty-three pence. The actual amount needed to carry out said repairs was in excess of fifty thousand pounds, so there was an obvious shortfall. It was a depressing situation that the young reverend found himself in to say the very least. Needless to say, things in the fund-raising department had hardly been going along in leaps and bounds, and due to this there were now whispers of possible demolition being imminent. The church, in their infinite wisdom, was considering selling off the land as prime real estate and pocketing the cash. The reverend and the small congregation were adamant that this was not going to happen if they had anything to do with it. Of course, in the real world, they didn't. It was now accepted that nothing short of divine intervention was going to save this little place of worship from the developers. As the Devil was only too familiar with both the church and its problems, it was towards this elderly domicile that he was now headed. The streets of London when near empty, as they were now, have always provided a singularly haunting quality, no doubt born of their extreme age and the countless number of people who have traversed their oddly intriguing by-ways down the centuries. True to say, the Devil didn't in any way feel spooked by it. If anything, he found it rather comforting. It was his kind of place.

Turning into Bernier Street, he proceeded at a pace. St Luciens was situated on the left, about two thirds of the way down. A small wall lay at its front, with the greater part of the render having now fallen away. A series of wrought iron railings, (the rust now being indistinguishable from the paint) adorned the wall, and these ran the length of the small enclosure. A tiny gravel pathway led to the church's front entrance. At one point in its past, the church had boasted an undersized cemetery.

This was during the reign of George the First. But, as space continually got ever scarcer in the old capital, it was taken over and those interred had been reburied elsewhere. No one quite knows where, as the records containing such information had been lost a very long time ago.

The Devil stopped outside the once black iron gates; his eyes immediately drawn towards a small wooden noticeboard. It advertised the following warning in large red letters: KEEP OUT. CLOSED FOR RENOVATION UNTIL FURTHER NOTICE. A death knell if ever I've seen one, he muttered beneath his breath.

Circling the two gates was a large imposing steel chain, joined at the front by a monstrously large padlock. It appeared quite anomalous, especially considering just how ineffectual it was for keeping anyone out. It was a simple case of anyone wishing to break in to merely stand on the little wall and then hop over – not that anyone would ever have considered it.

The church looked desolate, old and utterly abandoned, but the Devil knew otherwise. And so, he moved on.

To the right of the church, there lay a small narrow alleyway. It was towards this he now headed.

About halfway down the alley was a tall wooden gate. Knowing it would not be locked, he turned the handle, pushed it, and let himself in. Another gravel path led straight to an imposing, thick, oak wooden door. The Devil entered and then turned right into the vestry. Through a small side window off to the right, he could see a light burning brightly; a strange and unexpected effulgence given the current situation, and also not forgetting the lateness of the hour. A small door stood just ahead of him. Once again, he passed through, closing it quietly behind him. He ensured that he made great effort not to disturb the person he knew to be in the church to his presence.

Despite the small light, the church's interior was sombre, dimly lit and redolent of its former glory. The cold and dampness exuded from the very stonework and made the church's interior so cold it easily matched anything that might be expected to on the outside.

Slowly and with great stealth, the Devil made his way to the nave. There he saw a young man kneeling deep in prayer. It was all too apparent by the way he appeared to be in a constant state of agitation, as opposed to the serenity you might expect from someone engaged in such spiritual engagement, that all was not well with him. It was as if he were praying with the very intensity of his soul. The debilitating affect it was having on his wellbeing was only too apparent to see. He features looked drawn, tired and haggard.

Unsure as to just how long the man had been engaged in prayer, the Devil chose not to interrupt him, but decided to wait patiently until he had finished before engaging him in conversation. Patience was a virtue that the Devil possessed in immeasurable quantities. After all, it was part of his job.

Fortuitously, the man appeared to have completed his prayers after only a few minutes. Making some unintelligible comment, he terminated the session with an 'Amen', before rising and knocking the dust from his trousers. As he did so, his eyes alighted upon the Devil, who was now sitting in one of the pews. The shock of seeing anyone else in the church very nearly caused the poor man to experience a severe bout of apoplexy.

"What the b…" he began, before managing to get under control any expletive that may have possibly seemed fit to use at that particular juncture. "Do excuse me – I was altogether shocked and surprised at seeing anyone else here at this time of night. In fact, you shouldn't be here at all. Excuse my brusqueness, but the church has been designated unsafe. It's in need of structural repairs and is currently off limits to the general public. The whole place could come crashing down at any moment I'm afraid. Or, at least, that is what I am reliably informed by those in the know."

The Devil smiled and rose from his seat.

"But you're here," he said in a very courteous but disarming way.

This response seemed to catch the young man slightly off-guard.

"Well, well yes I am," he replied. "But I am entitled to be here you see. I'm Adrian. Noble, the reverend of this church."

"Ah, yes. I assume that would be the same Reverend Adrian Noble that is shown on the noticeboard outside?"

"Yes, one and the same. For my pains," he admitted.

The Devil gave the impression of giving the response some thought, and then finally observed, "But your title of reverend doesn't stop the place from falling down around your ears, does it?"

"Well, no, it doesn't," replied the Reverend Noble, trying to sound as patient as he could. "However, I am here for personal reasons, and I'm afraid I really must ask you to leave." He wasn't sure what the man was doing here. It wasn't as though he appeared to be a down and out, or even seeking shelter against the wintry conditions outside, (and heaven knows he had seen a few of those in the past); nor did he look the worse the wear for drink – having thought he may have been on the way home from a party, or some such. Could he merely be a lunatic? That's all he needed if it were the case. As if things hadn't been bad enough.

The Devil smiled and extended a hand in greeting. "You must excuse my apparent reticence, only I saw you were engaged in prayer and that you seemed heavily absorbed by it. I didn't wish to disturb you, so I chose to wait until you had finished. My name is Nicholas Bergdahl, by the way. I represent an organisation that deals in the – I wonder, before I go any further, is there anywhere we could go for a brief chat? I can then explain in full my purpose for being here? I will literally keep you no more than just a few moments. You have my word on that."

The reverend considered the man's request and thought it would certainly do no harm. The man didn't seem threatening in any way and what's more, he personally felt in the need for some human company. His recent exploits of late, with his continual late night of pray had left him feeling altogether drained and not to say isolated in the least. A chat with another person may be just the thing he needed to raise his spirits.

"Yes, of course, please come this way," he said. "I have a small room at the back, which I use as a sort of office from time to time. It's a little cluttered, and a bit untidy, but at least there's an electric fire there that should take the evening chill off to some degree. I have to say, being here night after night,

116

I tend to get used to the chilly conditions. At least on the up side, it never appears so cold outside when I am obliged to leave again."

The Devil allowed the reverend Noble to lead the way through the church, as he followed on close behind. As they walked, he asked, "Just out of curiosity, and I hope you don't mind my asking, but how is the fund raising going?"

The reverend Noble paused in his stride.

"Ah, a bit of a sore point is that I'm afraid to say," he replied. "In fact, it would be true to say that it isn't going well at all. When I first launched the campaign, so many months ago now, I can't even recall the exact date, I firmly believed that it would slowly pick up momentum. However, in truth it has all but fizzled out. It's all rather depressing and disheartening to be honest with you. Very dispiriting. But there we have it."

The Devil gave his commiserations.

"How very sad and unfortunate," he said. "I don't suppose the parishioners could really be expected to stump up such a large amount. No, that's not at all practical."

"Yes, what you say is true. They have done what they can, but we are still woefully short of funds. It's a great concern. Here we are. My office, for what it is worth. Please come in. And do please excuse the clutter."

They entered a small room, which as the reverend had just admitted, was indeed rather cluttered. But despite the mess, he found them two empty chairs and soon plugged in the single bar electric fire, which in truth did little to dispel the apparent chill of the place.

"Yes, as I was saying," he continued, "the parishioners are few and far between. I didn't really expect them to shoulder the burden. I have approached the local authorities for the required funding, along with various charitable organisations. Unfortunately, I have drawn a blank everywhere I have gone. It just makes things worse, as I feel I have let my parishioners down. Everything has had to be cancelled, as you might imagine. But we always had a good carol service at Christmas, without fail. Though it wasn't to be this year. Fate seemingly took a hand there."

Sympathising, the Devil said, "That is all rather sad. But surely, this is a grade two listed building is it not? Shouldn't it be preserved against things of this nature?"

"Yes, it is," replied the reverend noble. "But I am afraid it carries very little impact when weighed against the context of gain. Land within the city is of such a high premium, a small church is of little significance. And unfortunately, we don't have the necessary funding to prevent it."

"It seems to me as if you need a little divine intervention, or a miracle perhaps," said the Devil.

The reverend noble nodded in agreement, and then attempted a laugh that carried little conviction.

"That is precisely what we need; though in my experience genuine miracles are in very much short supply. I was in fact praying for one when you caught me just now. Truth is I've been doing that for some time if I was honest. I seriously believe the knees of my trousers are wearing so thin with all the kneeling I have been doing of late that I shall soon need a new pair soon."

The Devil inclined his head in understanding.

"I have little or no doubt that time will soon tell as to whether your prayers have been heard, and if a miracle is imminent," he said. "Faith, as they say, can move mountains."

It had to be said that the reverend Noble did not look entirely confident about that at all.

"Anyway, I believe I have dwelt upon my troubles long enough," he said. "It is Christmas after all. I believe I have a bottle of sherry around here somewhere. I could go and try and locate it if you would like a glass?"

The Devil thankfully declined the offer, saying that in general he didn't drink.

"Then I shall keep it for another occasion. Now, how exactly may I help you Mr Ber – was it Berd—"

"Bergdahl, corrected the Devil. It's of Swedish origin, on my father's side."

"Yes, yes of course, Mr Bergdahl. How precisely may I be of service to you?"

Rising, the Devil took out a manila envelope from his coat pocket.

"I think perhaps there is something here that you may find of particular interest," he said. "Look, I'm sorry to go off on a tangent like this, but I don't suppose there's a toilet I could use is there? I came away from a meeting earlier and I haven't had a chance to go. I'm a bit sorely in need."

"Why, of course. It's just by the exit, next to where you came in. On the right. There is a light switch by the door. Just pull the cord."

The Devil thanked him profusely and promptly left, leaving the reverend noble alone with the manila envelope. He examined it closely, turning it over in his hands several times. There was nothing printed anywhere that might give any indication as to what it might be about or where it was from. He prayed it wasn't any bad news, either from the local authority or the building contractor that had assigned to carry out the work. That was something he couldn't endure at present. He decided to take the bull by the horns, breathing deeply he quickly tore it open. Inside, he found it contained a letter printed on good quality note paper, no heading, no telephone number, no signature, nothing whatsoever that might have given it away. The few printed words that it did contain had been typed. It read:

'Dear Reverend Noble,
please find enclosed a cheque that should solve the greater majority of your problems.
Signed: A Well-wisher.

And that was it in its entirety. Returning to the envelope, he looked inside. There was a slip of paper. He took it out, only to find that it was in fact a cheque, and a banker's one at that. It was made out for the princely sum of sixty thousand pounds. The reverend stood staring at it in complete shock for some moments, hardly daring to believe what he was seeing. He checked the letter again for any sign of just who may have sent it, but there was absolutely nothing. A well-wisher? What well-wisher? Who could it be? He needed answers. Replacing the letter and cheque back in the envelope, he went off in search of the mysterious Mr Bergdahl. He would certainly be able to provide him with the necessary information he sought.

When he got to the toilet, he knocked gently upon the door and requested if everything was all right. There was no answer. He knocked a second time and waited, raising his voice slightly. Again, there was no response whatsoever. Slowly, placing his hand upon the door handle, feeling it was now essential to find out just who the generous benefactor was, he turned it and pushed the door open. Inside, everything was dark. There was no sign of his companion. None at all. The Reverend Noble was left shaking his head. He failed to understand exactly what had happened, given that Mr Bergdahl would have had to pass his office in order to make good his exit. And as the door to his office had been left ajar, he was sure he would have seen and heard him leave. More to the point, why would he wish to disappear like that? He had no answer to that question. But Mr Bergdahl had well and truly vanished as if he had been mist. It was as if he had never been at all.

Chapter Ten
A Brief Aside

The Devil was obliged to do something he rarely did if ever –
something that, in the main, was altogether anathema to him
– something, if truth be told, he hadn't done in many years
now; and, what is more singular, it was something he
absolutely loathed and detested doing. It was altogether
beneath him – it was something for mere mortals alone; he
was above that sort of thing. He was the Devil after all. But
the situation called for it and so he did it. He ran. He ran at an
altogether blistering pace, considering he was not used to it,
and what is more, that there was ice and snow everywhere,
which made running even more perilous. He shot across
Bernier Street and into the Charing Cross Road, turned left
passed the Crypt and made his way to the rear of St Martins-
in-the-Fields – the very place that Old Meg had used to
frequent not so long ago.

Almost at once, he knew that he was too late; he had
tarried too long; having been interrupted with his schedule
and having spoken with Michael earlier. Just as he arrived, the

clock tower above began to ring out the sound of midnight, its deep near sepulchral sounds filling the night air. There was no one else around; all had returned home by now – that is except for the dispossessed – and even most of those had escaped to whatever bolt hole they could find against the fierce wintry conditions.

Looking upwards, a look of shock horror on his face, he saw that he was indeed too late. His heart nearly burst with anger and the sheer frustration of it all. He had failed. Due to his own laxity and short sightedness, the worst possible outcome had occurred. There before him, hanging from the black wrought iron gates, was a young woman. She could only have been in her mid-twenties and was suspended from a piece of bright blue nylon cord, that now pulled tightly around her neck. Despite having been there for so little time, the intensity of the falling snow had almost covered her remains; it was as if nature itself was delivering a white shroud as a mark of sincere respect for the poor girl's passing.

The Devil gripped the railings and howled at the top of his voice. There was no one to hear him. And had there been he wouldn't have cared. He stood bereft and alone, looking up at her youthful, pathetic features, now set forever in a frozen attitude of death. This was not how things were meant to be! Life in all its glory, to be reduced to the ignominy of such as this! Such potential in a human soul, suddenly stopped dead in its tracks. A road no longer travelled, brought to a faltering and terminal end by despair and despair alone. And he should have been here to prevent it. That had been his job.

The railings vibrated alarmingly, as he gripped them forcibly and shook them in his terrible rage. He had the power within him to reduce them all to atoms in seconds, but in so doing it would have achieved nothing, not even so much as appeasing his own anger. He knew that and he also knew who he was, he knew his power, his purpose, his remit. And this was not it.

Standing upright, he finally composed himself sufficiently, and looked up at the girl's poor face. Then he swore an oath to himself. It would not end like this. He vowed it. No, fate would not have the final say here. Briefly, he placed a hand to his chin and began to rub his beard thoughtfully. He did this for at least a minute, ruminating as to what best he should do, what would be the best course of action to take – and more importantly, not forgetting any possible consequences of what that might be. There were always consequences and they were not always good, of this he was well aware.

"Not supposed to," he muttered, thoughtfully. "A bit unethical, I know…it upsets the scheme of things… Always does. Though saying that why should I care? I'm pretty autonomous, it has to be said. It is, after all, my decision and mine alone. And I stand or fall by it. So be it!"

Removing his glove, he pointed his forefinger at the clock face that stared down so sternly at him from the tower above and started to concentrate hard. Slowly and with great intent, he began to revolve his finger in an anti-clockwise motion. At first, nothing appeared to happen, then, all at once the minute hand of the clock began to move, ponderously at first, as it performed an action to which it was not intended – that of going in reverse. A quarter of an hour went by – then a half hour – and then a full hour! And then another and another. It continued in its ever-speedy progress until it showed exactly 6.25pm. The Devil replaced his glove and smiled. There was always more than one way to skin a cat. A trifle extreme admittedly, but it would achieve the desired result one way or another. He was confident about that.

The first thing that was apparent after completing his task was that the young woman had now disappeared entirely from view. There was now no sign that she had ever been there. The second, was that the general Christmas hubbub had returned in full vigour, it now being so much earlier in the evening. People walked the streets, celebrating to the extreme, eating establishments were still open and doing a brisk trade. All to the good, he thought as he turned to leave.

Within a short space of time, he had returned to the Strand. Looking in the direction of the railway station, he immediately spotted himself from earlier across the street, just arriving for the first time that evening. His other self looked up and also noticed him. The Devil nodded across to his other self, not desirous of a long and tedious explanation as to why he was here. His other nodded in response and then they both moved on with their respective assignments. Neither had seemed at all perturbed by witnessing one another as though it were a common occurrence.

It had to be said that there was no particular reason why the Devil should have travelled so far back in time. His current charge would not have required the amount of time he had allotted himself in which to turn things around and make things right again. And this he knew only too well. No, this was something he had decided upon on the spur of the moment. And as the old adage said, "One may as well be hung for a sheep as a lamb." And that was something he firmly agreed with. His choosing to return to the same point at which he had originally arrived at was purely to satisfy his own ends, to give himself a small amount of lee-way to indulge a little bit of his own personal vanity and also to re-establish some very personable and pleasant memories he had acquired down the centuries. It wasn't something he was usually prone to do. But on this particular occasion he did. And what better time to do it than in London on Christmas Eve?

He set off at a brisk pace along The Strand, stopping every now and then to look in shops, wish passers by a very Merry Christmas and just generally soak in the sheer magic of the time of year. All very decadent, especially as there was work to do – but he didn't care. This was now his time and he intended to make the most of it and woe-be-tide anyone that got in his way.

He had gone no more than two hundred yards when he saw coming towards him an elderly man. As soon as he saw him, he knew he had met this individual before, more than twenty years before to be precise, and it was a meeting he would sooner have not had, had the choice been his. Raising an eyebrow skywards, he muttered under his breath, "Yes, you've made your point."

The man, now in his eighties, carried a large wooden sandwich board. Written on the front of it were the words: **REPENT! THE END OF THE WORLD IS NIGH!** And beneath this in smaller script was written: **1 John 3:8 "Whoever makes a practice of sinning is of the devil, for the devil has been sinning from the beginning. The reason the son of God appeared was to destroy the works of the devil."**

He felt a huge sigh coming on. Every now and then, he was obliged to deal with people who appeared to go to the extreme in being wholly unaware of everything around them.

They cloistered themselves in ignorance and encouraged it to proliferate by the very nature of their unwillingness to open their eyes to what was real. And of all the people he should meet on this most prestigious of nights, it had to be someone who fitted this profile to the nth degree. The one person the genus Homo could perhaps not be applied, as it did amongst all the other bi-pedals that currently walked the earth. He knew he could, if he so wished, go around the man, ignore him and walk on and that would be the end of it. But he also knew that that was not really an option. He stopped in the middle of the pavement. The elderly man also stopped. They looked one another up and down. It was the Devil who spoke first.

"I believe it behoves me to point out to you my good man that there are numerous errors and misnomers in your rather odd, and not to say the least forbidding transcript here." And with that, he pointed towards the wording on the board.

The old man looked closely at him, altogether puzzled by this odd observation.

"Eh? Errors? What errors?" he demanded to know.

The Devil muttered the words 'Dear God' under his breath and once again pointed to the wordage on the board. "It's all wrong!" he said.

"What's wrong?" asked the old man, trying to view the words upside down.

"Well, to begin with, the end of the world is not nigh. I can assert with great confidence that it will continue on its elliptical trajectory for countless eons yet to come. You espoused this nonsense over twenty years ago. Total garbage then and it's even more so now. Only then it was the Mayans and the millennium bug! Or have you forgotten? We're all doomed, you forecast. But as it turned out, you were wrong then and you are equally wrong now."

The old man, not liking what he was hearing one bit, waived a belligerent and bony finger at him.

"It's the work of the devil!" he yelled loudly, causing those shoppers around him to give him a wide berth. "Repent – or you too will end up burning in hell with all the other sinners!"

Through pursed lips, the Devil responded.

"I'll decide on that if it's all the same to you," he said, feeling his ire rising by the second. "And what's more you've written the word Devil with small d. And as it's a proper noun, it should be written with a capital D. This is shoddy at best and I have to say that I find this personally offensive. I notice that you include the word God with a capital G. If you are going to promote this sort of wanton gibberish, for heaven's sake at least have the forethought to get it right!"

This dressing down caused the old man to view the Devil in a whole new light. And it was in a light that he didn't find comfortable with in the slightest. This wasn't the usual angry member of the public he was obliged to deal with, that much he was convinced of. This was something wholly different. And so, not having a rational answer to provide, he pointed the accusing finger yet again, only this time he made a stabbing motion with it.

"SINNER!" he howled. "You're the very DEVIL!"

"Yes, I have to say your powers of perception do you credit. However, I also have to say that I have had enough of this ridiculous badinage my aging friend. Let's cut to the chase, shall we? How about I show you something that I think may be of interest to you?" And so saying, he placed his hands

128

either side of the old man's head and stared with a remorseless intensity into his eyes. The old man's frame shook briefly, causing the sandwich-board to vibrate alarmingly, and then he went stock still. After a moment or so the Devil released him from the vice like grip he had had on the man's head and quickly moved on, leaving a bemused, near catatonic, old man to contemplate what had just been revealed to him.

As the Devil briskly moved along Fleet Street, with his good humour now fully restored, he could hear the old man behind him shouting: "I'VE SEEN THE LIGHT! I'VE SEEN THE LIGHT!" at the top of his voice. And it had to be said that he had in fact done just that.

The Devil, not intent on allowing his attention to be drawn away from his personal indulgences any further, left him to his own devices. The old chap seemed a lot happier for it. Everything else could now wait awhile. From now on, all his energies and efforts would be directed towards his own needs with what little time he had. It was his job, he knew, to extend a helping hand to all those who were deserving of it, but despite his true raison d'etre, it was important not to forget that this allotted time was his and his alone and no one else's; and if those upstairs didn't like it then they could lump it – plain and simple.

As he walked, he was determined to take in every colourful light, every shop, every piece of tinsel and every heart-warming sound that filtered through the ever-falling snow. Oh, how things had changed down the centuries, he thought. Shop fronts often came and went, but the buildings invariably remained the same. He personally had a liking for those of the Victorian era, being absolutely resplendent in their Gothic style, with a plentiful supply of stone carvings –

and a healthy preponderance for gargoyles and demons. They were put there as an ever-present warning to the unwary of what lurked beyond for those who failed to live a compassionate, thoughtful and caring existence. The thought gave him a warm, tingly glow all over. The Victorians certainly knew a thing or two about moral façades.

He stopped mid-stride, his gaze captured and enthralled by a sound that came from the other side of the street. It appeared that a group of people were holding a carol service, purely for the benefit of anyone wishing to take in the magical and melodic sounds. This was almost too much for him and he was obliged to take a handkerchief from his pocket and wipe away a single tear, one born of pure happiness and delight. Crossing the street to get a better look, he now saw the real reason for their communal efforts. Placed carefully before the group was a large plastic bucket supported by a metal tripod. On the bucket were the words **'SUPPORT THE NEEDY – PLEASE GIVE GENEROUSLY'.** Now this was what life was all about and he fully endorsed it with all his heart and soul. It saddened him immensely to think that so few of those individuals living, breathing and going about their daily lives failed to see the real reason for being here.

Having listened to half a dozen heart lifting carols – and having joined in with the odd one or two (the Holly and the Ivy being his personal favourite) he removed a glove and took out from his inner pocket a large wad of bank notes, before surreptitiously placing them in the bucket. One of the ladies, warmly bedecked against the evening chill, stopped singing and thanked him warmly for his contribution, unaware of the true amount deposited. He had in fact just dropped ten thousand pounds in newly minted £50 pound notes into the bucket. Thanking the woman most cordially for her good wishes, he turned and re-crossed the road – his heart beating in time with the music. Such joy.

His curious perambulations finally brought him to St Dunstans Court and then on into Johnsons Court. It was a place he knew well and one that appeared virtually the same as he remembered. He was looking for one domicile in particular. It was the former house of the great and renowned Dr Johnson.

And then there it was standing before him, seemingly unchanged, pristine and looking for all the world as if the man himself was still ensconced within. The small garden, the stone steps, the front door, it was just the same as it ever was. He stood marvelling at it for some moments, enthralled. How anomalous he thought, in this fast-moving world, where things appeared to change quicker than the weather, that here we had a semi-permanent bastion, a throwback to years gone by, just as it was all those years ago. It had hardly changed at all.

Standing here now as he was, staring up at the old house, all the memories began to filter back. It made him smile. The long and many varied conversations he had had with the great man in the past. Wonderful debates, angry disagreements, arguing about the very nature of everything under the son. Heady days, and he remembered them all with great joy. Naturally, the Dr had not been aware of his true identity, revealing that would have been the wrong thing to do. No, back then he was known as Dr William Pryce, a lesser known man of letters. But, saying that, hadn't it been his idea and his alone to compile a list of all known English words and publish them in the form of a dictionary? The very first dictionary in fact. Many was the time the pair of them had sat before a roaring fire indulging in semantics and imbibing best port. Oddly enough, the good Dr hadn't been too keen on the idea initially. It had taken a lot of effort on his part to induce him to make a start on it. And even then, he was obliged to lean heavily on the man's vanity and pride. It was odd, he thought, how few people nowadays actually remember who it was that wrote the first dictionary. He looked up at the house, which now seemed so out of place in the modern surroundings and smiled. Thoughts of the Great Fire came to mind and the ensuing conflagration. Not a time to be in the capital during that time and no mistake.

Strangely enough, the Lord Mayor, Sir Thomas Bloodworth hadn't taken the news of the Great fire all that seriously at first. On the night in question, his maid had woken him with the alarming news that there appeared to be a large orange glow across the east of London, that looked for all the world to be a large fire. She feared it could spell imminent danger to them all and so woke her master immediately. Sir Thomas resplendent in his night attire, had looked at the scene, announced it was so small that a woman could piss it out and promptly returned to bed. The following morning, history then showed just how wrong he had been, with over a third of the capital going up in smoke.

As the Devil stood in front of the house reminiscing as he was, it occurred to him just how pleasant it would be to have a look inside once again. Just for old times' sake. It certainly wouldn't do any harm, would it? And of course gaining access to the property would not cause him a problem. And, in addition to that, no one would be any the wiser for his visit, would they? Before you could blink, his mind had been made up, he would go inside.

With his intention now clear, he moved to push open the iron gate, but as he did so he heard a strange and altogether discordant noise coming from just around the corner. It was a sound that really had no right to be there at all, especially at this time of the year. It was a ragged, brutal sound, out of keeping with Christmas altogether.

Despite his foremost intention of taking some time out from his busy schedule, he reasoned that it might be wise to check it out. If it turned out to be nothing of importance, then he would come straight back. Pulling himself together, along with his thoughts, he strode the short distance to where the sound had come from. As he walked around the bend, a sight met his eyes that instantly made his hackles rise and his blood ignite. Lying on the ground was a middle-aged man, obviously destitute judging by his clothing. He was covered in blood, the greater majority of it now staining the snow all around him. The place resembled an abattoir. Above the prostrate man stood three youths; their belligerence exemplified in both their posture and the way they circled their victim, gloating in a way that sickened their onlooker to the pit of his stomach and his very core. They reminded him of a pack of vultures hovering above a newly dead carcass. The man had sustained such a savage beating he appeared unconscious, though this was not the case as his piteous groans could still be made out.

The Devil had seen enough. Moving quickly from out of the shadows, he stepped forward and confronted the three youths' head on.

"WHAT HAS THIS MAN DONE TO YOU?" he roared.

Straight away, all three of the youths stopped what they were doing and looked at him. The nearest one to him replied, "He didn't have to do anything mate – dirty filthy beggar! The place is better off without his sort. And what's to do with you anyway?"

The second then added, "Yeah, we don't want his sort around here! We don't want his filth cluttering up the place."

The Devil, ichor now coursing through his veins, stared at them intently and echoed the youth's words.

"Better off without his sort? And what precisely qualifies any one of you to decide what 'sort' the world is better off without?"

The third youth called, "Mind your own business, mate – unless you want some of the same. Clear off! You're out of your depth here, granddad."

Confrontation, such as this, on tonight of all nights, was not something he had factored into the time he had allowed himself. He resented it. He resented it very much. This was supposed to be HIS time! And those that impeded it would pay and pay dearly.

The Devil stepped forward, so that he stood directly in front of all three of them.

"Everyone one of you is a living testament to everything that is wrong with this world!" he bellowed. "You personify what is bad and your very existence creates an ever-increasing burden on society, a burden that I am obliged to ultimately shoulder. And it is like an albatross around my neck! And let me tell you that I resent it. I resent it to the very heart of my being!"

The three youths continued to stare at him in mute anger at having their fun disturbed, thinking that he must be out of his mind.

"I can see our friend here wants some of the same," said the first youth aggressively. At that, all three made a move towards him. The Devil merely smiled, knowing his power in such matters.

"Ah, gentlemen, I believe it so important that each of us realise their own limitations – don't you think?" he said without rancour. "The error of your ways, my friends, the error of your ways. Please let me have the pleasure of pointing them out to you – only in a little more graphic detail than you might usually expect. I sincerely believe that you will find it a very sobering experience!"

Before any of the youths could react, the Devil's appearance began to change, the earthly guise he had assumed fell away, revealing his true self in all its satanic majesty. As the three looked on, a universal horror at once overtook them. Not one of them spoke. The vision before them rendered them unable to utter so much as a word. And even they had been able to speak, there were no earthly words to possibly describe what they felt now as their sanity was brutally and irrevocably stripped away forever. All that was left was little more than a series of mortal shells, shells that were now devoid of virtually everything that had once made them human. Their on-going existence would forever and irrevocably consist of nothing more than a continual and sheer unadulterated terror clothed in flesh. All three of the youths turned and fled, making instinctively for anywhere that was away from that place. In seconds, the Devil and the beaten man were left alone.

Once they had gone, the Devil straight away assumed his previous appearance and bent down to see to the stricken man. As he had rightly supposed, the man had taken a vicious beating and had lost a lot of blood. He knew that he could endeavour to contact an ambulance; though given the time of year and the lateness of the hour, and not forgetting the very inclement weather, he reasoned it would be better to deal with things himself. In less time than it takes to think it, a medical bag had appeared before him, though he appeared to have no recourse to use it. Waving his hand above the stricken man seemed to provide for his entire medical needs: the blood disappeared, the abrasions and bruises vanished from sight. Where only seconds before the man had been semi-conscious, he now opened his eyes and showed signs of looking a whole lot better. He sat up unaided and asked groggily: "W…what happened?"

The Devil helped him to his feet and began to explain:

"You appear to have gotten on the wrong side of some yobs," he said. "When they saw me, they took off. Not sure why. I don't regard myself as being that intimidating. Can you walk? Here, let me help you."

"Yes, I think I'm okay now, thanks to you. Thanks for your help. I much appreciate it."

The Devil informed the man that it was really no problem at all and he had if the truth be known found chasing off the yobs quite liberating. He then went on to explain that he was a medical orderly on his way home and had just happened to hear the commotion and had come to see what was going on.

"I find it often pays," he said. "You never know when you can lend a hand. Why did they attack you like that anyway? What had you done to provoke them?"

"I made the mistake of asking for money," said the man. "Just a few coins, that was all. I've been experiencing a bit of bad luck lately. It's difficult enough living on the streets, but at Christmas time it's even worse. I thought, Christmas cheer and all that. It just might count for something. It would seem I was wrong. A bit naïve, I suppose. There's not much compassion about nowadays. People have too much else to think about."

"May I rightly assume that you have nowhere to go at present?" asked the Devil.

"That just about sums it up," replied the man. "Just trying to get by until things pick up again. Get back on my feet a bit. Well, you never know your luck, do you?"

Pursing his lips together thoughtfully, the Devil said, "You know I believe I may be able to help you there. Collect your belongings together and come with me a moment. If we hurry, we just may be in time."

As directed, the man collected what few items he had and followed the Devil out of the Court. They returned to the Strand and at once the Devil took off across the street with the man in tow. The object of his intentions were still there, just where he had seen them earlier – the charitable carol singers. They were in the process of packing up for the evening when the Devil intervened. He explained at length of the man's dilemma and precisely what he had endured, and then proceeded to make another sizeable donation to the bucket. The carol singers all gathered around both of them, all full of the Christmas spirit. They were only too pleased to help, explaining that they would ensure that the man was well cared for. After all, wasn't it their duty? The charity's sole purpose was to help the needy, wasn't it?

Feeling very satisfied that his job there had been done, the Devil wished the man well and went on his way. He had no time to exchange pleasantries any further. Time was fast ebbing away and there was one last place he wished to visit before he was obliged to continue with the job in hand.

Chapter Eleven
The Last of the
Dispossessed Peggy

Making his way through the traffic, the Devil crossed the road once more and made his way along Fleet Street. He was intent on returning to an inn, though nowadays it such establishments were more commonly known as a bar. It was a place that he had frequented many times over the centuries. It was known as Ye Old Cheshire Cheese and had stood at number 145 Fleet Street for as long as people could remember. It had a rather unromantic name and was, to be honest, a rather unromantic place. It was said that all the furniture, settles, chairs, tables etc. were the original ones from when the place was first built. Not that it mattered of course. The place was somewhere that held some very pleasant memories for him and he intended to try and relive a few of them again before the evening inevitably came to a close.

When he finally arrived at his destination, he found that the whole place was heaving to the rafters. There were so many customers present, those that had managed to get served were standing outside, glass in hand, not giving a hoot about the snow or the cold weather. They were just intent of having a good time no matter what.

Despite the place being so crowded, the Devil had little or no trouble making his way to the bar. It was as if by magic, people just miraculously moved away to one side to let him through, feeling that he was probably before them in the queue. Customers lined the entire length of the bar, all waving bank notes in the air in the vain hope of being served. The staff were rushed off their feet, hastily moving to and fro, with the sound of the cash register ringing loudly in the background as if it were doing its very best to wake the dead.

Waving his own bank note high, the Devil was served virtually immediately, much to the chagrin of a young well-dressed man standing next to him who had been standing there trying to get someone's attention for well over twenty minutes.

"My, I wish you'd show me how you do that," he said, good humouredly. "Can you believe it, I've been standing here for ages now, and with no sign of being served. It's next to impossible. Whatever you are doing you need to get a patent on it fast, because you certainly have the knack. You'd make a fortune."

Joining in with the man's laughter, the Devil replied, "It's just a question of who you know."

"The devil himself I shouldn't wonder," replied the man.

"Yes, something like that," returned the Devil. "Here, let me buy you a drink. It will save you waiting all evening. No, put your money away. This is my round. A very merry Christmas to you. I'm Nick by the way."

"Peter," said the man, thanking him for his generosity, as the barman brought them two glasses of the best Old Barley Mow ale. "Your very good health, sir – may your life be long, fulfilled and blessed by the Almighty."

"Well, nearly right," muttered the Devil beneath his breath and followed it up with, "and the very same to you, sir. Good health."

They touched glasses and then Peter asked, "Busy here tonight and no mistaking. Mainly office workers catching a skin-full before heading off home. Do you mind if I ask what line of work you are in?"

No one had ever asked him that particular question before and he was obliged to give the question some serious thought before responding. He finally gave an answer that was as close in proximity to the truth that he could think of.

"Acquisitions mainly I suppose – oh and arbitration, of sort or another. It's a pretty autonomous position really. No one to answer to in the main – well, within reason," he replied, with a certain amount of half-heartedness thrown in for good measure.

"Sort of self-employed, eh? It all sounds pretty interesting," Peter replied.

The Devil grinned broadly.

"Oh, it can be. I'll say that. It certainly has its moments."

"I'm in Futures myself. It pays well, but the pressure can sometimes get to you. Very often I just need to get away, have a quiet drink and slow my thoughts a little – though that's not really feasible here tonight, is it? What precisely do you acquire by the way?"

The Devil prevaricated again and then changed the subject.

141

"Did you know that this place is positively seeped in history?" he said. "So much so it's in the very brickwork."

"Well, I know it's been around a pretty long time, though precisely how long I couldn't say. I don't come in here very much. And history has never really been my strong point. I do believe GK Chesterton used to drink here on and off, or so I'm told."

The Devil nodded.

"That is very true. Along with Charles Dickens, Mark Twain, Alfred Lord Tennyson, Sir Arthur Conan Doyle and not forgetting Dr Johnson. It really has quite a pedigree."

Peter looked impressed.

"Wow, it certainly sounds like it. I hear they say Dr Johnson was a real character, a bit of a tartar by all accounts. Would have been great to meet him."

Smiling, the Devil replied, "Well, if truth be told, he was a genius, there was little doubt about that, but he was also arrogant, self-indulgent, self-opinionated, pig headed, a bit of a prig, altogether larger than life – oh, and he didn't suffer fools gladly. And he used to sit just over there if my memory serves me correctly. Same table too by the look of it."

Peter looked at the Devil sideways.

"You make it sound as though you knew him," he said laughing loudly.

"Did I?" said the Devil feigning mild surprise. "I read an awful lot. I think what I meant to say was his greatness seemed all encompassing. It really shone through, or so I've been led to believe."

And so, the conversation went on for some time in this vain, the Devil providing stories and anecdotes about what had transpired hereabouts over the centuries. Peter listened avidly, taking in everything that was said, not sure if the Devil was making most of it up, even though it certainly sounded most genuine. And he certainly had no wish to openly doubt the man by questioning his integrity.

It was at this point the Devil took out his pocket watch and consulted it, appearing genuinely surprised by the passing of the time.

"Oh dear. I'm afraid I must be going. There's someone I need to see. Second time this evening. I unfortunately missed them earlier. It was bit remiss of me to be honest. But I can't afford to make the same mistake twice. As an aside, did you know that the owners of this establishment used to have a grey parakeet here many years ago? It lived in a cage just over there on the counter. Its name was Polly. Not very original, I know. Scurrilous little blighter it was too. The language that issued forth from its beak was nothing short of appalling. It was that bad it would have put a fishwife to shame. Even taking that into account, it still had a universal appeal, which made people come from far and wide just to see it. Created quite a stir when it died."

Peter found the recollections fascinating and roared with laughter at this one.

"It sounds as though it was quite a character. Did they replace it when it finally popped its clogs?" he asked.

"Apparently not," replied the Devil. "I imagine they didn't think another one would fill old Polly's boots by all accounts. The bird's still here by the way. He's just over there in a glass case. Looks a little ragged and moth eaten now, as you might expect after all this time. It's still nailed to the perch or so I'm informed. A bit brutal perhaps."

"That's a little macabre, isn't it?"

"Yes, I suppose it is. But then the whole place is a tad macabre, don't you think?"

"It's not haunted, is it by any chance?" Peter asked.

"Who can say? It certainly wouldn't surprise me for one moment if it was. Now, as I said, I really must be going. People to see and all that. It's been nice meeting you."

He quickly downed the remainder of his beer, placed his glass on the counter, wished Peter the compliments of the season and left.

Standing outside the pub, the Devil turned up his collar, patted the brickwork lovingly and then made his way along Fleet Street towards Trafalgar Square. This was going to be his final effort of the evening, that is assuming nothing untoward was going to occur like earlier. The vicissitudes of life – they never ceased to amaze.

As he stood waiting forever patiently, just across the street from Charing Cross station, he consulted his pocket watch for the umpteenth time that night. It was becoming a bad habit with him, and he must try and get out of it.

"I'm definitely getting too long in the tooth for this sort of thing," he grumbled, and gazing into the heavens added, "time for a reprieve perhaps? Or maybe something along those lines?" He waited. The only response he received was that the ever-falling snow now appeared to increase in its severity. Replacing the pocket watch into his coat pocket he mumbled "No, I thought not. A little Christmas spirit wouldn't have gone amiss."

He was so wrapped up in his quiet conversation with the powers that be he was totally unaware of someone approaching him. The person touched his arm.

"Hello again. Who were you talking to just now?"

The Devil turned to see the young Asian woman from earlier. This was an altogether shock and for the briefest of moments he was lost for words. Then he quickly reasserted his calm demeanour and smiled.

"Well, well, well. What an altogether pleasant surprise. I must say I didn't expect to see you again so soon."

The young woman looked at him a trifle confused.

"I don't fully understand how it is I left you only a few minutes ago. You were waiting for your friends. And yet you are here before me. How is that possible?" she asked.

Knowing that the truth was the last thing she would have been able to accept as an answer, the Devil instead replied, "Ah, yes. Had a call. Just after you left me. They got a little delayed. That's life I suppose. But no worries. I will deal with them later. It is Christmas after all."

"But how did you get here before me?" she pressed. "You certainly didn't pass me. If you had, I would have seen you."

"Oh, I simply cut through Northumberland Street. Fact of the matter is I do walk at quite a pace. I've only just arrived here. Lovely to see you again."

The young woman didn't look too convinced by what he said but didn't question it. How could she, he was here after all. Instead, she simply asked, "Are you waiting for someone else?"

The Devil nodded.

"Er, yes, I am," he replied. "She will be here very shortly now."

She smiled.

"The I will let you get on with your waiting. Don't get too cold, will you?"

Once again for the second time that evening, they both wished one another the compliments of the season and the young woman left him alone. He was grateful that she hadn't decided to return to the embankment. If she had, then she would have been confronted by the site of him dealing with Ed, Barry and Razors. Now that would have taken some explanation.

As he continued to wait, he watched the people passing by and wondered how different the world would be if everyone was to suddenly Wake Up, instead of going about their daily lives in a semi-somnambulistic state, as most people so often did. If that were to happen, it would undoubtedly put him out of a job. What a gratifying thought. Of course, he had suggested something along these lines eons ago – and look where that had gotten him. It sometimes paid you to keep schtum, and merely go along with the grand plan, that which was commonly known as the 'ultimate scheme of things', amongst those in the know that is. Either way, there was still plenty he hadn't been made party to. And he doubted whether things would ever change in the foreseeable future. He would continue to carry on regardless, until the powers that be decided otherwise. And when that was precisely meant to happen, he couldn't even begin to imagine. If truth be told, he was usually the last one to find out about things.

The minutes ticked slowly by, and he amused himself while he waited by staring through the window of a bar next to where he stood, viewing all those within. He enjoyed people-watching; he always had. It usually endorsed what he already knew about the human race, their frailties, their odd peccadilloes, their fears, hopes and dreams. As he gazed through the window, his eyes alighted upon two young men who were apparently becoming rather heated in their discourse, about what he knew not what. More to the point, he didn't really care. The same scenario was playing itself out all around the globe, over and over and would continue to do so until there was a universal awakening. He wanted to shout 'WAKE UP!' at the very top of his lungs, but the Grand Plan didn't call for it. He would continue to do his job, as he always did, and that would be the end of it. No one, at least, could call him an iconoclast.

Then all of a sudden something told him that his final meeting that night was nigh. Looking up, he saw, through the ever-falling snow, his ultimate assignation. She was walking calmly towards him, looking neither impoverished nor down at heel, not like the majority of the dispossessed he had met that evening. Instead, she appeared completely vacant, utterly distraught and she walked in a near lifeless and mechanical fashion.

She kept her face bent down against the driving snow, but in truth appeared oblivious to it. The Devil knew it was definitely her all right, the self-same young woman that only earlier in the evening had been suspended by her neck from the railings of the church at St Martins in the Field. Not that anyone would have recognised her though. But he certainly did. As she got ever closer to him, he could see that she carried a small knap-sack with her. It was not large, though definitely large enough to contain what he knew it to contained. It was time to put his plan into action.

He purposefully moved in front of her and blocked her progress; the young woman moved aside, as if to go around him; but he moved to his right to block her path again. She promptly apologised and moved to her right to avoid him. He, casually moved to the left, again blocking her way. This time, she stopped briefly and looked up, and once again moved sideways to avoid him, thinking it was just a mistake. Once again, he did the same.

"W-What's y-your p-problem?" she asked irritably. "L-L-Let me by. I'm in a h…h…hurry."

Looking at her closely, the Devil saw that the girl had a severe nervous tick and it was all too apparent. Her right cheek constantly twitched, as if it were being continually being subjected to numerous electric shocks. She also looked and sounded extremely neurotic. Not a good combination, he thought. A walking disaster of a human being if he'd ever seen one. Pulling out a warrant card from his inner pocket, he pushed it into her face and then said, perhaps a trifle more sternly than he should have.

"Peggy Manders? I'm Detective Chief Inspector Valentine from the Metropolitan Police. I would like to talk to you about your possible involvement in the death of a young woman."

Peggy stood shell-shocked. She instantly froze and looked for all the world as though her deepest most innermost secret had been exposed to the whole world. She also looked as if she were about to pass out.

"W…w…what?" was all she could utter in her traumatised state.

"I believe you heard me well enough the first time," the Devil continued, perhaps once again a little harsher than he actually intended.

Peggy experienced a numbness from top to toe. She was not responsible for the death of anyone, and she knew it. She'd never knowingly hurt anyone in her entire life. This policeman had made a mistake, a terrible mistake. Yes, that's what it was – it was a genuine mistake. Surely, she could make him understand and then go away and leave her to it. He had to believe her. Now was not the time to be delayed by issues that had no bearing on her life. She had something she had to do and it couldn't wait.

"Y-Y-You've made a m-m-mistake," she finally announced, knowing that her voice carried no conviction and didn't at all sound anywhere near convincing enough. But then, it never did, despite the fact that she had done no wrong. Her facial tick began to increase in rapidity. It always did when she felt under any form of stress or pressure. She hoped the policeman hadn't noticed. Discreetly, she placed her hand across that part of her face, trying to give the semblance that she was guarding herself against the driving snow. The Devil continued to stare at her intently, which made feel even more ill at ease. She found it very unnerving and wished he'd just go away.

"I rarely make mistakes," he said, confidently. "We can discuss this matter at greater length down at the station. I'm afraid you will have to come with me."

This was the last thing she wanted to hear.

"B-B-B-But you d-don't understand," she stammered. "I h-have to b-be somewhere – it's important."

"Oh, do you now? Well, you will just have to cancel it, won't you? You're coming with me, and it brooks no argument – that is unless you would like me to hand-cuff you and march you there for all the world to see? The choice is yours. It doesn't bother me in the slightest."

Peggy felt crushed. This was all she needed. Tonight of all nights. Earlier she didn't think the day could get any worse.

How wrong she was. Feeling utterly broken, her head slumped forwards.

"V…very well. I will g…go with you," she said.

The Devil smiled triumphantly.

"That's gratifying to learn, young lady. It never pays to argue with the law. Let's go this way, it's a short cut."

And so he led her in the same direction he had come just a short time earlier, retracing his steps, until he finally arrived at the very same spot where he had found her body hanging from the railings, not so very long ago. He stopped and looked at her enquiringly.

"Are you familiar with this place?" he asked pointedly.

She was, very familiar with this place. It was the very place she had chosen in which to – in which to… How did his man appear to know of her intentions? Surely, it must be a coincidence? None of what was happening here made any sense – none of it.

"Well?" he pressed, giving her little or no time to consider.

"I sometimes come here during the day," she confessed. "When things get a little too much to – when I need a little quiet time, I find it peaceful. It helps me to think better."

"It's certainly peaceful," he admitted. "Though not so peaceful at this time of night on Christmas Eve, especially when there's something akin to an ulterior motive. Wouldn't you agree?"

Looking the policeman full in the face was something she couldn't manage, so she merely nodded. He appeared to know her thoughts, her motives and her intentions. How was that possible? She shuddered at the thought of it.

"Can we leave this place?" she asked at last, feeling the oppression beginning to overwhelm her.

"I think that would probably suit the both of us, don't you?" he replied. "Anyway, I'm starving. I've just realised that I haven't eaten anything all day. Let's go and get a bite of something – I know of this small bistro just around the corner. Food's great. We'll be there in under two minutes. I used to frequent another one just across the way there, but it's gone now, turned into a stationary shop or other I believe. Pity that. Come on! Look lively. Step out!"

And off he went at a pace, leaving a mightily confused Peggy to trail in his wake. This was the strangest policeman she had ever encountered. Of that there was no question. It was a complete mystery to her precisely how he came by his information, which she found uncanny and unnerving. As she endeavoured to keep up with him, she managed to ask, "I thought we were going to the police-station? That's what you said."

Giving her a brief backwards glance, he answered, never once slackening his tempo, "Why would we be doing that?"

"But you said I was under arrest," she persisted.

"If you believe that, then you are under a misapprehension! Think back. What I actually said was I wanted to speak to you in connection with your possible involvement in the death of a young woman. And I for one would prefer to do that in the warm confines of somewhere that sells good food, and what's more, somewhere that sells food to my liking."

She felt more confused by his behaviour by the minute. What did this all mean and where was it all leading?

"So, I'm not under arrest then?" she asked.

"I never said you were," he replied. "Do listen, and please try and keep up."

In very little time, they had arrived at what indeed was a small bistro, just off the Charing Cross Road. It was tucked well away from the main thoroughfare and looked quaint and most select. The Devil pushed open the door and entered, allowing Peggy to follow. At once, a waiter appeared, smiling and ushered them to a table.

"I can recommend everything that is on the menu," said the Devil in a lively manner. "The soup in particular is exceptional and the bread is made fresh on site. It's to die for."

"I'm not hungry," said Peggy miserably.

Giving her one of his sourest looks, the Devil said, "Humour me."

Finally, she agreed to a bowl of soup. If it kept him happy then hopefully, he would get to the point, which would then allow her to move on.

The waiter took their order and then left them alone.

Peggy sat opposite him and looked about her. They were the only ones in the restaurant, which she found a trifle odd, considering it was Christmas Eve. The place should be packed, over flowing with customers, not empty like this.

"Not many people in here," she finally remarked.

The Devil smiled.

"No, a bit off the beaten path this one – and naturally people have celebrating to do, parties and what not. Personally, I'm glad of the quiet and the seclusion. It gives me the ideal opportunity to talk to you in relative peace and quiet about the matter in hand, don't you think?"

Once again, she was on her guard.

"Talk to me about what?" she asked him defensively.

Placing his head slightly to one side, he looked at her keenly. It made her uncomfortable.

"Why you, Peggy. What else is there?"

Peggy didn't like the sound of that at all and thought it best to try and take the conversation to him.

"You said I had some involvement with the death of a young woman. I can tell you that I haven't, not now, not ever. I know absolutely nothing about whatever it is your going on about."

"Well, is that right?" he asked and leaned forward across the table.

"Yes, it is," she answered.

Slipping his hand into his coat pocket, he took out an envelope and placed it before her.

"If that's your stance, then I seriously suggest you look at these. They say otherwise and in fact tell a very different story," he said without betraying any emotion at all.

With great hesitancy, Peggy picked up the envelope and removed the contents. She held up a series of photographs. They were all taken from different angles and showed herself suspended from the iron railings, though due to the heavy snow it wasn't easy to determine who the person actually was. A wave of nausea spread through her. In shock and horror, she dropped the photos on to the table.

"Who is this?" she asked, not daring to think for one minute that they could in the least bit be genuine.

The waiter arrived with their soup, leaving the Devil to wait until he had gone before continuing with the conversation.

"Ah, the transitory nature of life, don't you know? You don't recognise her then?" he asked.

"No, no I don't. They're horrible photos. I don't know why you would wish to show me such things. I had nothing to do with this," she said. "Nothing!"

"Is that a fact? Well, I disagree. I think you know exactly what I'm getting at. Look again, only look a little more closer this time."

"I don't wish to. They're horrible!"

"Yes, I couldn't agree more," he replied. "They are indeed horrible. Believe me, it's even worse when you're close up front and on the receiving end of something like this. But then those people who carry out this sort of thing rarely give any thought to those they leave behind, do they? Those I mean that have to clear up the mess. Go on, have a closer look – I insist!" le pushed the photos beneath her nose and waited. Reluctantly, she picked them up again and went through them one at a time.

"I don't know what you want me to say," she said uneasily. "As I said before, they are horrible photos."

"Does anything ring a bell with any of them?" he asked. "Anything at all? lave a really good look."

"No, they don't mean anything to me, why should they?" She was beginning to get near hysterical. What did this man want from her?

"Why indeed? Let me ask you, what's in the bag by the way?"

"Bag? What do you mean?"

The Devil pointed to her knapsack.

"Pretty standard question. What's in the bag?" he pressed.

"Nothing – there's nothing of any importance – just some personal things, that's all. A change of clothing."

"Then you won't mind showing me then, will you? The change of clothing, I mean."

He held out his hand for the bag, which she reluctantly and after much deliberation handed to him. Opening it, he pulled from within a lengthy coil of bright livid blue nylon rope. There were no clothes as she had claimed. Peggy's face fell.

"Funny change of clothing, don't you think? And, er, precisely how did you intend to wear this? Christmas party with a bit of a twist, was it?" he asked.

"It's nothing," she replied unconvincingly.

"Then if it's nothing, may I suggest that you pay close attention to the photos yet again, and also the length of rope from which this poor unfortunate is dangling? Pay REAL close attention."

Once again, she looked at the photos. After a moment, her face turned ashen. She dropped the pictures on the table and stared intently into his eyes.

"You aren't a policeman, are you? I know that. I don't know who you are, or what you are, but you most definitely are not a policeman. Tell me who are you? And tell me the truth."

Collecting the photos up, the Devil placed them in the envelope and replaced them in his coat pocket.

"You know, Oscar Wilde once said 'The truth is rarely pure and simple', and he was right. Let us say that I am someone with a vested interest in seeing that you stay alive," he replied. "And we can leave it at that. I insist."

"I don't understand. How come you have a vested interest in me?" She wanted to know.

"Sometimes it is better not to divulge the real truth in order to spare the one who would hear it. It is better I just tell you this: retain what you have and treasure it, for it is not yours to take. And now I have a gift for you."

"A gift? What gift?" she asked, feeling most confused by the sudden change in his attitude towards her.

"It is a gift that has already been bestowed," replied the Devil, and he took from his pocket a small mirror and handed it to her. "Here, look closely and tell me what you see."

Feeling even more confused, she did as he asked, but could see nothing irregular, just her own face looking back at her.

"What am I supposed to be looking for?" she said feeling a little foolish by it all.

"It's not so much what you are looking for, but more what you not seeing," he said. "Look again, only a little more closely this time."

Peggy looked again – and then it dawned upon her. The realisation hit her full force, like a train travelling at one hundred miles an hour.

"My God! It's gone! My facial tick has gone! I can't believe it! low – How did you – How did you do that?"

The Devil waived a hand dismissively and smiled.

"Oh, it was nothing miraculous I can assure you," he said. "A helping hand, no more. I merely eased a small burden. And each and every one of us has one or two of those. Oh and incidentally, you will also find that your stammer has now left you. Again, a bit of a leg up. Nothing to write home about."

And it had! In the confusion of all that had transpired, it hadn't even occurred to her that she no longer had a stammer. She was speechless and was left staring at him, mouth hanging all agog. The Devil simply dismissed it with another half-hearted wave of his hand.

"It's time, I feel, to move on to pastures anew," he said. "I should eat your soup before it gets cold. And while you are eating you can enlighten me with your story. I feel sure it is worth listening to. Take your time, believe me when I say I'm in no hurry."

Her head still reeling from everything that had transpired, Peggy proclaimed that she had no story to tell. "I'm just ordinary," she said and she genuinely believed it. "There's nothing special about me. People tell me often enough."

The Devil shook his head sadly.

"A truth that is told with bad intent, beats all the lies you can invent," he said.

Peggy confessed to not understanding exactly what point he was making, so he explained further.

"You know, it is easier to believe a lie we have heard a thousand times than a truth we have heard but once. Your problem up till now has been you have spent too much time believing other people's lies and paying little heed to their misguided opinions. They have become so entrenched in your state of being you now actually have complete and utter faith in something that is not real – to whit, what everyone else thinks about you. So again, I repeat, tell me your story."

And so while they consumed their hot soup, Peggy told him of how her low level of self-esteem had plagued her for more years than she could remember. It had become like a lead weight, which oppressed her constantly without let up. Things had come to a head the day before. She had lost her job, without warning, and then. to make matters worse, had also lost her place of residence as she could no longer pay the rent. Her one and only friend had been obliged to return home due to it being Christmas, which meant as she had no family, she now had nowhere else to go. It was at that point she had decided to end things. Life simply wasn't worth living any longer. Or so it had seemed.

The Devil listened intently and with a sympathetic and favourable ear.

"You will be amazed just how short a period of time it takes for the whole picture of life to change," he said. "Sometimes, when it happens, it is near miraculous."

No sooner had he spoken when Peggy's phone rang. It made her jump.

"I should answer that," he advised. "It could be important. I'm just going to settle the bill with our friend over there."

Peggy took the call. It turned out to be her very good friend Allison. The same one who had chosen to go home for the Christmas holidays. It turned out that, for reasons unknown, she had chosen not to return home after all. What this meant was she was now at a loose end for the Christmas period. Peggy explained her current situation and her friend told her to come over immediately. They could spend the holidays together.

Feeling as though the weight of the whole world had suddenly been lifted from her shoulders, Peggy rose to inform the man of her good fortune, (whose real name she still didn't know). But when she looked for him, he was nowhere to be found. He had apparently gone. She went across to the waiter, who stood behind the counter and asked if he had seen him. The waiter replied that the man had paid the bill, left a sizeable tip and had then left. Before his departure, he had handed him a folded slip of paper and told him to give it to her before she left. The waiter then did so. She quickly moved to the door, opened it and looked out. There was absolutely no sign of the man anywhere, not even so much as a single footprint in the snow. She looked at the piece of paper that she had been given and quickly opened it. The sheet contained the following words.

'Be in the world, not of it. Or, in short – Be passer-by.'

Chapter Twelve
The Final Farewell

Standing on the forecourt of Charing Cross Station, for the final time that evening, the Devil removed a glove and raised a hand to the ever-falling flurry of snow. A number of flakes adhered to his hand, but for some inexplicable reason they refused to melt, almost as if they wished to show themselves off to their new observer in all their frozen wonder. The Devil smiled for one last time, though a little ruefully. It was time for him to go. "Magical," he said quietly, voicing his thoughts. Blowing the flakes from his fingers, he then proceeded to remove a pencil and a small notebook from his pocket. Opening the notebook to the required page, he slowly began to place a tick against the names of all those he had visited that evening and then made note of a couple of additions. Just as he was placing the last of the ticks, he became aware of another presence just slightly to the right of him. Adjusting his gaze, he saw standing approximately twenty yards away a man dressed virtually identical to himself; the only difference being was that the man's hair and beard were almost preternaturally white. The man did not speak, but merely raised a hand in acknowledgement and then gave an almost imperceptible nod in the Devil's direction. The Devil, for his part, did not speak either, not feeling the need, but simply raised an informal eyebrow as greeting. He watched as the man turned and began to walk slowly away. Very soon, he was lost amongst the falling snow. The Devil replaced the pencil and notebook in his pocket, clapped his hands together as a final parting gesture and began the short journey into the station.

As he was about to enter it, he remembered something he had forgotten. Taking out his pocket watch he looked at it closely. "How remiss of me," he muttered. Then adjusting the hands on his watch, he returned time to what it should be again. Once accomplished, he replaced the watch in his pocket and patted it with satisfaction. "We don't want to leave any loose ends now, do we?" he said.

On the way into the station, he encountered an elderly couple who were in the process of coming out. They appeared most distressed and were all of a bother. As they passed him, they stopped and spoke.

"There are no further trains tonight," said the woman sounding most distraught.

"Apparently, there's a points failure somewhere or other. There doesn't seem to be any information. We don't know what we are going to do."

"Oh deary me," said the Devil. "Well, that's going to make it rather tricky for people wanting to travel home again, don't you think?"

"Yes," said the man. "And that was our last train too. The Devil knows what we are going to do now. It's too far for us to walk and it will cost a small fortune for a hotel – and that's if could even find a room this time of night."

Turning, the Devil raised a hand and pointed to just across the way from where they stood.

"That's no great problem," he said. "There's still a taxi or two hovering about if you look for them. I know for a fact that there's one over the road there, just to the left of the bus stop. Can you see? Go and ask for Sid. He will see you home safely and he doesn't over charge. I guarantee it."

The couple, hardly believing their good luck, thanked him profusely, then wished him the compliments of the season and turned to go. The Devil returned their wishes of good will, waved them goodbye and slowly entered the station.

Had anyone been on the station's interior at that precise moment, then they would have been hard pressed to see him come out the other side. He had simply gone the same way he had arrived earlier that evening – in a puff of smoke.

Chapter Thirteen
And What Happened After

Nigel

The warmth of the train on the ride home slowly seeped into Nigel's bones. It was only when faced with the simple luxuries of life did it bring into clear focus what it was like to spend any time on the streets. Taking out the envelope that the social worker had given him, Nigel counted the money it contained for the third time. There was exactly one thousand pounds in crisp, newly minted, fifty-pound notes. It seemed an awful lot of money. He could only assume that it was a new government incentive or some such, introduced to get people off the streets. If so, then it had certainly worked in his case. Once he was home, he intended to put it to good use. He also intended to change himself for the better, be more flexible – and try and bend a bit more, as the social worker had said. The thought gave him a warm feeling. Upon reaching Bradley train station, he was a little surprised to find that there was no sign of his family. The social worker had definitely told him that they would be waiting for him. Perhaps there had been a mix up of some sort. He wasn't overly concerned by this, as his parents' house was situated only a short walk away and he could be there in no time.

Having covered the short distance very quickly, Nigel knocked excitedly on the door and then waited. Despite the lateness of the hour, there were still lights on within. He was glad of this. They were obviously waiting for him. Within a moment or so, the front door opened to reveal his father, whose jaw promptly dropped upon seeing his errant son once again. His mother then appeared in the doorway, to add to the further jaw dropping. There was much emotion shed. This was married with tears, along with great excitement at the return of the prodigal son.

It had to be said that his family seemed unaware of any social worker as he claimed. Certainly, they had not been contacted by any authority, local or otherwise. Nigel was of the opinion that it was no doubt down to a bureaucratic cock up back at the office. Ultimately, it didn't really matter. It was Christmas and he was home with his family again and that was all that mattered.

Meg

Meg had felt very special, her being chauffeured through London in a large black car. It was something she was not used to. It made her feel rather important. The driver hadn't spoken a single word, not once throughout the entire twenty minutes or so the journey had taken to arrive at their destination. She thought this odd but lapsed into a cosy silence of her own as she was enjoying the experience so much. It made her feel like royalty.

Upon their arrival, she found that the hotel was just as it had been described by Nick. Her items were carried safely inside and she was shown to a small but pleasant room on the ground floor. Over the Christmas period, she met many of the other guests, all of whom appeared to have come from the streets, just as she had done – all courtesy of Nick. Sitting around and doing nothing, however, was very much discouraged and everyone was expected to chip in and pull their weight. This entailed making things in the small workshop, which were later sold for the benefit of local children's charities. No one minded, as this made them feel as if they were actually giving something back and they were not left feeling a burden on the establishment.

After Christmas, Meg was given, as promised by the Devil, the opportunity to return to her place by the baker's. She chose not to.

The Professor

On Christmas Day, during the afternoon, after a particularly filling and satisfying lunch, a young couple were traversing the snowy streets of central London when they began the long haul from Embankment to the Strand. As they passed by Victoria Gardens, they happened upon the note left the previous day by the Devil. Upon reading it, they immediately contacted the police, who arrived on the scene rather quickly given the time of year. The professor's body was then taken away for examination. As he had been homeless, it was usual practice, in case of a death, to bury them in an unmarked pauper's grave – even in today's enlightened times. However, a curious benefactor had by all accounts paid in advance for him to be interred at Highgate cemetery, with no expense spared. It was said that even professional mourners had been hired for the occasion. Either way, the old man had been given a right royal send off. One of which he would have been altogether pleased with.

Ed, Barry and Razors

Initially Ed, Barry and Razors had no idea at all where they were, or more to the point how they might have got there. It all seemed very strange, and what's more they didn't recognise anything at all. They all agreed that the heat was rather oppressive – and whatever was causing the odd smell was making all their eyes water. Their individual memories were sketchy in the extreme. Not one of them could actually remember where they were before they arrived here, or precisely what they had been doing. Razors was adamant that they were on their way to a party, whereas Barry was equally convinced that they had in fact already been and were on the way home again. Ed, on the other hand, disagreed with both of them, stating that he was sure that their current memory loss was down to some bad stuff that they had all taken and it was only a matter of time before they all woke up again and things would get back to normal. They had wandered around for some time, trying to come to terms with their surroundings and trying to make out where all the apparent distant screams seemed to be coming from. None of it made any sense at all. Up until now, they hadn't seen another living soul. They had spent what had seemed like an eternity wandering aimlessly along a road that appeared to be going nowhere. The landscape either side of the road was bleak and without vegetation of any kind. Eventually, they approached a crossroads, which gave them all hope of finally being able to locate somewhere they hopefully recognised. Razors then pointed out what appeared to be a signpost. Their hopes rose even further. Hastily making for it, they were all altogether alarmed to see that each sign on the post pointed to the same place – 'HELL'.

May

During the ride home, May and her parents discussed at great length who the so-called Private Detective may have been, and, more to the point, where he promptly disappeared to when they had arrived. Her mother was insistent that neither herself nor her stepfather had hired one – but wished in hindsight that they had, as it had been a very good idea, or so they thought. The conclusion they finally came to was that the man, whoever he was, must have been some sort of a well-wisher and perhaps even knew the family, or he may have been a philanthropist of some kind. May wasn't so sure, after all, he had shown her his credentials – and there was not forgetting the letter supposedly written by her mother – which she could have sworn was written in her mother's own handwriting. It was certainly all a great mystery and no mistake.

Laz, Dominic and Lucy

Just as the Devil had promised, the private ambulance whisked both Dominic and Lucy away, and they received the best medical care you could imagine. Despite being at death's door, Dominic did in fact make a good recovery. Once fit enough, both he and Lucy joined a program that helped them reintegrate back into society. They were finally weaned off the drugs and life began to look good again. As for Laz, well his ending was altogether different. With his pocket bulging with the Devil's money, he was only too glad to go and dole out a bit of hallucinogenic Christmas cheer to anyone who would buy it. Despite already being paid well paid for his services by the Devil, he thought it a good idea to try and get his three friends to cough up a bit more money for what he had to offer. Nothing ventured nothing gained, or so he thought. True to his word, he found the Devil's colleagues lounging against the river wall. Knowing all their names, he dispensed with all formalities and introduced himself straight away, putting great emphasis on what he had to offer. He was a little more than taken aback when all three of them turned around and regarded him closely. The shock of seeing their near zombie like appearance he found altogether horrifying; even though it had to be said in his line of work he was used to seeing some pretty awful sights. No, the worst aspect of it was none of them appeared to have any eyes at all, only black empty sockets. He had no idea precisely what they had previously taken, but it must have been some pretty potent stuff to do that to them. Anyway, a deal was a deal. Taking out what he had, he proffered it to the three guys standing before him. They appeared to have less interest in that and more interest in himself, as they all three made a grab for him. It wasn't easy determining precisely what it was they were after, as they man handled him aloft. Despite his protestations and screams they continued in this vein, ignoring his shouts for help, until they finally hurled him bodily into the Thames. They then, one by one, all three promptly followed suit – for the second time that evening.

Miriam

Miriam's tale is of a somewhat sadder nature. After the Devil had left her, she took herself and Tigger off to bed, having worked herself up into quite a state by the solicitor's news. For long hours that night, she brooded over her husband, his passing, though more importantly on his spending every last penny they had. The thought festered in her mind and her heart. She had no remorse over his passing, none at all. In her opinion it was the best thing that could have happened. But if only he had held onto the money, or at least some of it, then she wouldn't have to continue living in this damp corridor.

A few days later, the firm of solicitors dealing with all the loose ends of his estate sold the property for a tidy sum and donated the proceeds of the sale to a number of local charities – as per the instructions in his will. Unfortunately, despite the solicitors being aware of the fact that he had a wife, all attempts at tracing her had come to nought. After the required amount of time had elapsed, as according to law, the proceeds of the estate were all given away.

Michael

Michael's Christmas turned out to be a series of agonising episodes of severe conscience. All the time he had endeavoured to put on a brave face and try and put his indiscretion behind him. It had to be said that he didn't find it at all easy. But then, as the Devil had pointed out to him, this was his penance and punishment and his alone and he would continue in this vain until he learned to forgive himself. Which it had to be said he wasn't finding at all easy. Naturally, this had been a life affirming lesson for him and, what is more to the point, one that he decided he would learn from and never stray from the straight and narrow ever again. And what's more, he never did.

The Reverend Adrian Noble

The Reverend Adrian Noble's Christmas had been a rather good one. Having returned home that evening, he had found his wife to be still up and awaiting his return. Upon being told of his good news, she too thought it a miracle. They felt truly blessed. After the Christmas period was over, they both made stringent attempts in order to locate their generous benefactor, Mr Nicholas Herdhaal and whoever it was he represented. Needless to say, their efforts were totally in vain. The money, as might be expected, served its true purpose and paid for all the restoration requirements. Within a few months, life at St Lucien's was back to normal, and with an even larger congregation than before. And as for the Reverend Adrian Noble, well, as he had suspected, the knees to his trousers had indeed become threadbare due to all the kneeling in prayer that he had carried out over the previous few months. Fortunately, there was sufficient money left over to enable him to purchase a new pair.

Peggy

As she sat upon the train that evening travelling the short distance to her friend's flat, Peggy gave long and serious thought to precisely what had taken place that evening. It was all rather muddled. She went over the events again and again in an attempt to make some sense of it all. In the end, she just gave up trying. Ultimately, it made no sense at all, everything that had occurred was outside the parameters of the known world in which she lived. Taking out the piece of paper left for her by the man, she read it again, (having read it numerous times before): 'Be in the world, not of it and Be Passer-by.' She wasn't sure what it meant. Well, whatever, she had little or no doubt it would all make some kind of sense in the end. After arriving at her station, her friend was there to meet her. Almost at once she noticed something about Peggy that was very near impossible to pin-point. A definite change had come over her, and it was a change for the good. Something about her general demeanour and an apparent new-found confidence perhaps. Who could say? As they walked back in the snow, Peggy took out the coil of bright blue nylon rope from her bag and consigned it to a nearby rubbish bin. When asked why she was throwing it away, she replied, "I don't have any use for it anymore."

A Final Thought

And that my friend is the end of this little Christmas tale.
And of the moral that goes with it? Never judge a book by
its cover.